Diana could only imagine what it would be like to wake up in an alien world, without friends or familiar landmarks.

Steeling herself, she fought the urge to lift a hand and stroke his cheek. He hadn't asked for comfort or condolences, and probably wouldn't appreciate either.

"Why don't we sit down, Major Stone?"

She took a single step, only to come up short as two palms slapped the wall beside her head. His arms caged her. His body formed an immovable wall.

"I want a few answers first."

"All right. But just so you know, this type of primitive behavior went the way of the poodle skirt."

Stone remained silent for so long Diana had to fight the urge to fidget. He was too close and too…too male. To her surprise and considerable annoyance, her skin tingled under her silk long john gripped her belly.

Dear Reader,

Valentine's Day is here, a time for sweet indulgences. RITA Award-winning author Merline Lovelace is happy to oblige as she revisits her popular CODE NAME: DANGER miniseries. In *Hot as Ice*, a frozen Cold War-era pilot is thawed out by beautiful scientist Diana Remington, who soon finds herself taking her work home with her.

ROMANCING THE CROWN continues with *The Princess and the Mercenary*, by RITA Award winner Marilyn Pappano. Mercenary Tyler Ramsey reluctantly agrees to guard Princess Anna Sebastiani as she searches for her missing brother, but who will protect Princess Anna's heart from Tyler? In Linda Randall Wisdom's *Small-Town Secrets*, a young widow—and detective—tries to solve a string of murders with the help of a handsome reporter. The long-awaited LONE STAR COUNTRY CLUB series gets its start with Marie Ferrarella's *Once a Father*. A bomb has ripped apart the Club, and only a young boy rescued from the wreckage knows the identity of the bombers. The child's savior, firefighter Adam Collins, and his doctor, Tracy Walker, have taken the child into protective custody—where they will fight danger from outside and attraction from within. RaeAnne Thayne begins her OUTLAW HARTES series with *The Valentine Two-Step*. Watch as two matchmaking little girls turn their schemes on their unsuspecting single parents. And in Nancy Morse's *Panther on the Prowl*, a temporarily blinded woman seeks shelter—and finds much more—in the arms of a mysterious stranger.

Enjoy them all, and come back next month, because the excitement never ends in Silhouette Intimate Moments.

Yours,

Leslie. J. Wainger
Executive Senior Editor

Please address questions and book requests to:
Silhouette Reader Service
U.S.: 3010 Walden Ave., P.O. Box 1325, Buffalo, NY 14269
Canadian: P.O. Box 609, Fort Erie, Ont. L2A 5X3

Hot as Ice
MERLINE LOVELACE

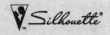

INTIMATE MOMENTS™

Published by Silhouette Books

America's Publisher of Contemporary Romance

 SILHOUETTE BOOKS

ISBN 0-373-27199-9

HOT AS ICE

Copyright © 2002 by Merline Lovelace

This edition published by arrangement with Harlequin Books S.A.

® and TM are trademarks of Harlequin Books S.A., used under license.
Trademarks indicated with ® are registered in the United States Patent
and Trademark Office, the Canadian Trade Marks Office and in other
countries.

Visit Silhouette at www.eHarlequin.com

Printed in U.S.A.

Books by Merline Lovelace

Silhouette Intimate Moments

Somewhere in Time #593
*Night of the Jaguar #637
*The Cowboy and the Cossack #657
*Undercover Man #669
*Perfect Double #692
†The 14th...and Forever #764
Return to Sender #866
**If a Man Answers #878
The Mercenary and the New Mom #908
**A Man of His Word #938
**The Harder They Fall #999
Special Report #1045
"Final Approach...to Forever"
The Spy Who Loved Him #1052
**Twice in a Lifetime #1071
*Hot as Ice #1129

Silhouette Desire

Dreams and Schemes #872
†Halloween Honeymoon #1030
†Wrong Bride, Right Groom #1037
Undercover Groom #1220

Silhouette Books

Fortune's Children
Beauty and the Bodyguard

†Holiday Honeymoons:
Two Tickets to Paradise
"His First Father's Day"

Harlequin Historicals

††Alena #220
††Sweet Song of Love #230
††Siren's Call #236
His Lady's Ransom #275
Lady of the Upper Kingdom #320
Countess in Buckskin #396
The Tiger's Bride #423

Harlequin Books

Renegades
"The Rogue Knight"

Bride by Arrangement
"Mismatched Hearts"

*Code Name: Danger
†Holiday Honeymoons
**Men of the Bar H
††Destiny's Women

MERLINE LOVELACE

spent twenty-three years as an air force officer, serving tours at the Pentagon and at bases all over the world before she began a new career as a novelist.

Be sure to watch for *Once a Hero,* the next book in the exciting new CODE NAME: DANGER series, feturing Jack Carstairs, code name: Renegade, coming soon in Silhouette Intimate Moments.

Merline enjoys hearing from readers and can be reached by e-mail via Internet through Harlequin's Web site.

This is for my dad, who flew high and flew proud.

Prologue

"*I hear her!*"

The figure swathed from head to foot in bright orange Extreme Cold Weather gear whooped with joy. "She's punching through!"

His companion spun in a circle, searching the endless, unbroken surface of the polar ice cap. A dozen different shades of white dazzled his eye, shielded though they were by protective goggles. The blue white of the ice. The downy, cloud-soft drifts of glistening snow. The hazy, gray white of the sky that merged with the horizon.

"I don't hear anything!"

"Listen!"

The frustrated listener threw back his hood. He

risked losing an ear to biting wind that dropped the outside temperature to almost thirty below but was too eager to care at that moment. Then he, too, gave a shout of glee as a series of sharp cracks rifled through the air.

Suddenly, a scant forty yards away, the ice cap erupted. Huge white slabs pushed upward. Groaning, they rose straight into the air before toppling over with a crash. A moment later, the tip of a black conning tower poked through the crack.

"How do you like that! She's right on target."

Both men grinned. Sophisticated navigational equipment had guided the USS Hawkbill *from Hawaii, but good old-fashioned muscle power had provided her surfacing site…a large X shoveled in the ice.*

The two oceanographers raised their hands and clapped fur-lined mitts in a jubilant high five. After months at the remote laboratory one hundred and sixty-five miles north of Point Barrow, Alaska, they were ready—more than ready!—for a fresh infusion of supplies and outside conversation. Still grinning, they watched as the submarine's conning tower rose a foot. Two feet. Ten.

The hulking body of the sub appeared, rolling great chunks of ice off its sides. When the hatch atop the conning tower opened and a hooded sailor appeared, the two men rushed forward.

"Boy, are we glad to see you!" the senior sci-

entist shouted. "We're down to the last battery for the underwater observation buoy."

"We brought the spares you requested." Bulky and awkward in his protective gear, the seaman climbed down the iron rungs riveted to the conning tower. "We'll start unloading immediately."

"We'll help. Jack, bring up the snowmobile."

Eager to get the valuable equipment unloaded and hauled back to the collection of huts connected by air-heated tunnels that formed the United States Arctic Oceanographic Research Station, the lead oceanographer threw an impatient glance over his shoulder.

"Jack! The snowmobile!"

His partner didn't move. Frozen in place, he gawked at one of the huge slabs of ice tossed up by the sub.

"What's got into you, man?"

His breath clouding on the frigid air, the senior scientist stomped across the ice. Irritation creased his forehead under his ski mask.

"Why are you just standing there? We've got a hundred tasks to get done before we... Oh, my God!"

His eyes bugged. Disbelief rose up in great, choking waves to close his throat, cut off his breath. Stumbling to a halt, he gaped at the helmeted figure staring back at him through five feet of ice.

Chapter 1

An early June breeze frisked through the streets of Washington, D.C. Trees decked in bright chartreuse dipped and swayed like synchronized dancers in the afternoon sunshine. The hundred-year-old chestnuts lining a quiet side street just off Massachusetts Avenue, deep in the heart of the capital's embassy district, whispered the same playful song. Their rustling branches almost obscured the facades of the Federal-style town houses that marched along either side of the brick-paved thoroughfare.

The town house halfway down the block presented a dignified front very similar to its neighbors. Three stories, with tall windows sparkling in the summer sunlight, the elegant one-time residence boasted a discreet bronze plaque beside the front door. The plaque confirmed that the dwelling now served as the offices of the president's special envoy…a nebulous position created years ago as a reward for a campaign contributor with a yen for a fancy title and a burning desire to rub elbows with the political elite.

Only a handful of Washington insiders were aware that the special envoy also served as the head of OMEGA, an organization so covert that its agents were known within the highest government circles only by their code names. Just as OMEGA represented the last letter of the Greek alphabet, this organization represented the U.S. president's last resort in a crisis. Its operatives were activated only when other, more conventional agencies like the State Department, the CIA, and the military, couldn't respond to a crisis for legal or political reasons.

The president himself appointed OMEGA's director. With great reluctance, he'd recently named a new chief, as the current head had requested an extended leave of absence. After directing the agency through three administrations, Maggie Sinclair had decided to take some time off to complete a ground-breaking book on infant phonetics. She also planned to add a third child to the large, chaotic household she shared with her husband, her two daughters, an overgrown sheepdog and a bug-eyed, blue-and-orange striped iguana with an appetite for paper and plants.

Her husband fully endorsed her decision and had recently resigned his own position as the U.S. ambassador to the World Bank. While Maggie worked on her book, the wealthy, sophisticated Adam Ridgeway had decided to try his hand at full-time fatherhood.

Every agent not currently on assignment or otherwise detailed had gathered in OMEGA's third floor control center to wish them well. Ignoring the soft chorus of beeps and blips emitted by the electronic communications consoles, they toasted Maggie and Adam as they began the latest phase in their hectic, adventurous marriage.

"The betting is you'll be back within a month," a lean, lanky operative with the code name Cowboy predicted. "One or the other of you. Hunting terrorists or illegal arms dealers is a lot easier on the nerves than raising kids."

"You should know," Maggie retorted. "Most couples would have the sense to stop after two sets of twins."

"What can I say?" Nate Sloan grinned. "This ole boy doesn't shoot blanks."

Amid the hoots and groans that followed, Elizabeth Wells calmly made the rounds to refill champagne glasses. The gray-haired, grandmotherly woman had served as personal assistant to the director of OMEGA since its inception. She was loved and respected by all for her many talents, not the least of which was her deadly skill with the 9mm SIG Sauer pistol she kept within instant reach at her desk downstairs.

Maggie waited until Elizabeth finished topping off the glasses to step forward. The irreverent grin that had both irritated and inflamed her one-time boss tugged at her lips as she tipped him a quick look.

"I'll admit I'm looking forward to spending more than two nights in succession in the same city, not to mention the same country, with my husband."

The answering gleam in Adam's blue eyes was for Maggie alone. She melted inside, and the muscles low in her belly clenched in delicious anticipation.

"As the president stated when he approved my successor," she said a little breathlessly, "I'm leaving OMEGA in good hands."

Her glance shifted to the operative standing quietly to one side.

"Nick is one of our own. Adam and I would trust him with our lives. We *have* trusted him with our lives."

Nick Jensen, code name Lightning, strolled forward and lifted Maggie's hand to his lips with a charm that fluttered every female heart in the room.

"It was my pleasure, Chameleon."

Straightening, Nick included her husband in his glance. Despite the differences in their ages and backgrounds, the camaraderie between the two men showed clearly in the smiles they exchanged.

"I'll never forget that breakfast on the veranda of the Carlton Hotel."

"Nor will I." Grinning, Adam clapped a hand on the younger man's shoulder. "I believe the bill for that journey of gastronomic discovery ran to three figures."

Maggie caught the curious looks the other operatives traded. Only she, Adam, and the couple who'd adopted Nick knew that this cool, imperturbable agent had once roamed the back streets of Cannes.

Surveying him now, Maggie found it hard to believe that a skinny, half-starved pickpocket with the improbable name of Henri Nicolas Everard had once graciously offered to serve as her pimp. Or that the bone-thin street tough kid would grow into such a hunk!

His boyish shock of red hair had softened over the years to a burnished gold. The wide, muscled shoulders covered in whisper-soft gray cashmere could have belonged to a linebacker. In fact, he'd traded his shorts and beat-up soccer shoes for a football uniform when Page and Doc Jensen had brought him to the States.

Fiercely loyal to his adopted country, Nick Jensen

had been educated at UCLA and Stanford. After graduation, he'd parlayed his early, ravenous hunger into a string of world-class restaurants that had made him a millionaire many times over. The outrageously expensive watering holes attracted movie stars and princes. They also allowed Nick to roam at will between the glittering world of the superrich and the dark underworld of terror and intrigue.

Which, in Maggie's rather vocally expressed opinion, made the tall, wickedly handsome operative the perfect choice for acting director of OMEGA. Happy to be leaving her team in such capable hands, she lifted her glass.

"*Bonne chance,* Nick."

"Thanks, Chameleon," he said in the rich baritone that gave no hint of his French roots. "I'll need more than luck to manage this crew."

"You've got that right."

Nick's gaze traveled over the small crowd. He'd gone into the field with most of these operatives at one time or another, had depended on their unique talents to get him out of some decidedly uncomfortable situations. Now he'd be the one to send them into harm's way.

He rolled his shoulders under his hand-tailored jacket. Nick hadn't asked for the director's job, wasn't sure he wanted it. He'd been his own man for so long that he'd balked at the idea of assuming responsibility for the dozen or so highly skilled and very independent OMEGA agents. But as Maggie so bluntly put it, the order to put your life on the line went down a whole lot easier when it came from someone who'd done just that countless times.

"Just don't take too long to write your book," he urged. "I'm opening a new restaurant in Lima in a few months, another in Acapulco later this year."

"Strategically placed to cover the Pacific drug routes," Adam murmured approvingly.

"Among other activities."

Maggie's brown eyes sharpened. She might have one foot already out the door, but the other was still planted firmly in OMEGA's control center.

"What kinds of activities, Lightning?"

He'd opened his mouth to relay the rumor of a high-seas pirating operation based in the Chilean capital when a shrill buzz cut through the air. Everyone in the control center spun around. In a room crammed with the latest in high-tech electronic wizardry, only one device broadcast that particular signal.

"I've got it!"

Mackenzie Blair, OMEGA's chief of communications, leaped for the central console. Slapping her left hand down on a flat surface, she snatched up a receiver with her right. Instantly, a complex double helix appeared on the screen above the console. Like colorful snakes performing some exotic mating ritual, the two strands writhed and danced for several seconds before confirming Mackenzie's DNA signature. Only then did the unscrambler built into the receiver activate.

"OMEGA control." Shoving a strand of her thick, unruly sable hair behind her ear, she listened for a moment. "Yes, sir. She's right here."

Turning, she offered the receiver to Maggie. "It's the president. He wants to speak to the director."

Maggie caught herself just in time. With a wry grin, she gestured to Nick. "It's for you, Nick."

"So it is."

He strolled across the room. OMEGA's chief of communications hesitated for the merest fraction of a second before handing him the receiver. Hiding a frown, she stepped aside.

Maggie Sinclair, code name Chameleon, had hired Mackenzie fresh out of the navy over the objections of some of OMEGA's older heads. Even more to the point, Chameleon had given her new Communications chief a blank check to procure the latest in high-tech gadgetry. She'd even sent Mackenzie into the field to experience first-hand the challenges of communicating with headquarters while dodging bullets or burrowing into burning desert sand to escape detection. Mackenzie considered Maggie her mentor, her role model, her friend. She still hadn't recovered from the shock of hearing that her idol was turning over OMEGA's reins for an indeterminate period.

And to Nick Jensen, of all people. An unabashed, unapologetic sensualist. An epicure, whose sophisticated palate demanded the finest wines, the freshest delicacies, the most glamorous dinner companions. In Mackenzie's mind, those qualities tended to blur the fact that Nick, code name Lightning, was also one of the most experienced operatives in the agency. She'd wasted two years of her life on a man with similarly varied, if decidedly less discriminating, appetites. Her ex had forever turned her off too-handsome, too-charming rogues.

Still, when OMEGA's new director pinned her with an intent stare, it took her a moment to get her breath back. And to realize he wasn't looking at her, but through her.

"Where's Artemis?"

Her glance flicked to the computerized status board projected onto the far wall. One of her unit's main challenges was keeping track of OMEGA's agents twenty-four hours a day. A single glance confirmed the status of Dr. Diana Remington, code name Artemis.

"She's at John Hopkins, teaching a class on antipeptide antibodies...whatever those are."

"Contact her. Tell her I want her in my office in thirty minutes."

Mackenzie's brows lifted at the preemptory order.

It hadn't taken Lightning long to shift from operative to director mode.

"Aye, aye, *sir!*"

A glint appeared in Nick's dark eyes. Deliberately, he planed the brusque edge from his voice. "While we're waiting for Artemis to arrive, get the Field Dress folks working on Arctic gear for her. Also, pull up everything in the computers on the U-2."

"The spy plane?"

"The spy plane."

Adam Ridgeway smiled as another "Aye, aye, *sir,*" rifled through the control center. Sliding a hand under his wife's arm, he squeezed gently.

"Strange how much that woman reminds me of one of my very best agents," he murmured.

"She should," Maggie replied smugly. "One of your very best agents personally trained her."

She took a last look around the control center, then set her champagne aside. Laughter danced in her eyes when they locked with her husband's.

"Let's blow this joint. The new team has work to do, and we've got a book and a baby to make."

A half hour later, Diana Remington faced Nick across an expanse of polished mahogany. In her ivory silk blouse and navy blue suit with its slim, calf-length skirt, she defied the stereotypical image of a molecular biologist. In Nick's considered opinion, she looked even less like an undercover operative.

As her code name suggested, however, Remington's silky, silvery blond hair and elegantly tailored suit belied her unique talents. Artemis was the Greek name for Diana, the Roman goddess of the hunt. The modern-day incarnation seated across from Nick was every bit as skilled as her mythical counterpart at tracking and bringing down her prey. This time, it appeared, her prey had already been found.

Diana's green eyes were wide with astonishment as she stared across the table at Nick. "They discovered *what* in the ice?"

"The body of an air force pilot."

"One of ours?"

"We think so. There are no identifying labels of any kind on his flight suit or helmet. That's a significant factor in itself. Additionally, the age of his equipment helped pinpoint his identity. All evidence indicates he's Major Charles Stone, whose plane disappeared from radar screens at 2235 Zulu on November 2, 1956."

Diana let out a low whistle. "He's been lost for more than forty-five years?"

"Apparently so. No trace of him or his plane were ever found."

"Didn't the air force mount a search and rescue operation when he went down?"

"They couldn't." Nick's dark eyes held hers. "His aircraft had just entered Soviet airspace when it disappeared from radar."

"Oops."

"Exactly."

The tip of Nick's twenty-four karat gold Mount Blanc pen tapped the cover of a plain manila folder. The pen was a gift from Maggie and Adam. The folder contained the data Mackenzie Blair had hastily milked from the OMEGA's supercomputers.

"If this pilot is in fact Major Stone," he continued, "he was flying a U-2, known in the air force by the nickname of Dragon Lady. It's a high-altitude, all-weather surveillance aircraft developed in the early fifties to collect data on Soviet ICBMs."

"I saw something about it on the History Channel a few weeks ago," Diana said. "Isn't that the plane Francis Gary Powers was flying when he was shot down over Russia in the early sixties?"

"It is," Nick confirmed. "Although the U.S. insisted the U-2's were only collecting weather data, the Soviets put Powers on trial for espionage. He was convicted and sentenced to ten years in prison, but exchanged after serving only two. The incident gave Eisenhower a political black eye and put Kennedy at a real disadvantage in the court of world opinion when the Cuban missile crisis came along."

Diana leaned back in her chair and played with a strand of her shoulder-length blond hair. Far too busy to waste time primping in the mornings, she'd be forever grateful to the savvy stylist who'd talked her into a wash-and-go spiral perm and a few age-defying highlights.

Not that she worried unduly about her age. At twenty-nine, she was one of the youngest biologists at the prestigious Harrell Institute, a private, non-profit consortium of scientists chartered to help define medical and moral standards for genetic research.

It was her *other* job that had carved the character lines at the corners of her eyes, she thought wryly. OMEGA tended to plunge its agents into situations that sent the pucker factor right off the charts. From the expression on Nick's face, she had a feeling his first official act as the new director of OMEGA would definitely have that effect on her.

Sure enough, Lightning tapped his shiny gold pen once, twice, all the while shooting her a considering look. When he tucked the pen into his suit pocket, Diana braced herself.

"The president is scheduled for a summit meeting with the new Russian premier next month. He isn't particularly anxious to reopen an old, embarrassing chapter in U.S.-Russian relations prior to the meeting."

"No, I can see he wouldn't be."

"Nor does he want to unnecessarily inflame certain right-wing groups in this country who still see

Russia as the evil empire and are looking for any excuse to resume the Cold War. If the Soviet Union shot down Stone, as they did Powers, relations between Russia and the U.S. could get real tense, real fast.''

''No kidding,'' Diana murmured.

''That's why you're heading north. Your civilian credentials give you the perfect cover to take part in the recovery operation. If the team of other scientists already en route to the Arctic Circle succeeded in breathing life into this iceman, we want you there to—''

''What!'' Diana bolted upright. ''They're going to thaw this guy out?''

''They're going to try. Apparently the body is perfectly preserved.''

''It can't possibly be *that* well preserved! Cyrogenics isn't my specialty, but I know frozen cell technology hasn't advanced far enough yet to undo damage caused by forty plus years buried in ice.''

''The Dragon Lady flew at such high altitudes that their pilots wore the equivalent of space suits. Dr. Irwin Goode, who worked the U-2 program during its inception, thinks the pressure suit may account for the remarkable state of Major Stone's body.''

Since Goode had been awarded the Nobel Peace Prize some decades ago for his pioneering work in the superoxygenation of living microbes, Diana refrained from arguing the point.

"Is Goode part of the team headed for the Arctic?"

"He is. So is Dr. Gregory Wozniak, who, I've been informed, recently cloned an ice-age mouse found in a cave in northern Siberia from a single strand of its fur. If Goode and company can't revive Major Stone, Wozniak wants to try cloning him."

Diana shook her head, both repelled and excited by the possibilities. Tremendous advances occurred in the field of genetics every day. Just last year paleoarcheologists had unearthed a frozen, stone-age mammoth and had hopes of crossing its DNA with that of a modern-day elephant. Still, for every step forward, there were a number taken back.

"Best I recall, Dr. Wozniak's clone lived all of two days," she said slowly.

"If this one lives two hours, you're going to be right there beside him, holding his hand." Nick's gaze drilled into hers. "The president wants everything about this man kept absolutely secret until we ascertain the facts surrounding his plane's disappearance. In the remote chance they actually bring Major Stone—or some version of Major Stone—back to life, we want you to act as his handler."

"But..."

"He'll be confused, frightened. Your job is to get

next to him, Artemis. Win his trust, find out what happened all those years ago.''

''All right. When do I leave?''

''An air force C-21 is standing by at Andrews, fueled and ready for takeoff. I advised the pilot that you'd be there in an hour.''

''An hour!''

Diana gulped down an instinctive protest. She had planned to have dinner with Allen tonight. She'd already cancelled twice this week.

She consoled herself with the reminder that Allen McDermott was a brilliant, dedicated scientist in his own right. Although he knew nothing about Diana's work for OMEGA, he understood that the pressures of her job at the Institute often required her to back out of their dates at the last minute. Allen would understand.

She hoped.

Flipping the folder shut, Nick slid it across the desk. ''This file includes a complete background dossier on Major Stone—his academic reports, military records and a psychological profile. By the time you reach the Arctic, you'll know all there is to know about the man.''

Diana had plenty of time to digest the file while a sleek, twin-engined C-21 ferried her to Eilson Air Force Base, just outside of Fairbanks, Alaska. There she boarded a four-engine turbo-prop C-130 Hercules equipped with skis.

When she finally climbed out of the 130, air chilled to a lethal twenty below by howling winds slashed at the eye and mouth slits in her ski mask. Dazzling blue-white light shimmered on the vast sheets of snowy ice, almost blinding her. Clumsy in her five layers of thermal underwear and outer Extreme Cold Weather gear, she waddled to the similarly bundled driver who zoomed up on a snowmobile just as the C-130 touched down.

"Welcome to the Arctic, Dr. Remington. Climb aboard and we'll get you out of the wind."

Huddled behind the driver, Diana skimmed across the packed snow to the collection of modular, boxlike buildings that constituted the U.S. Arctic Oceanographic Research Station. Once inside, she stripped off the bright orange cold weather jumpsuit and most of her layers.

"Diana!"

Greg Wells hurried forward to greet her. Short, bald, and radiating unbridled excitement, he was the world's leading expert on cyrogenetic regeneration. Diana had met him before at conferences and wasn't particularly impressed.

"Dr. Goode and I were thrilled to hear you were joining us," he said, pumping her hand. Without giving her a chance to do more than catch her breath, he swept her down a narrow corridor crowded with boxes and equipment. "I know you're anxious to view the find. He's right in here."

A few moments later, Diana stepped into a frost-coated storage annex and almost fell over her boots. She stumbled to a halt, mesmerized by the body stretched out on a metal table.

He was naked, bathed in harsh white light from head to toe, and absolutely the most magnificent male specimen she'd ever seen.

Chapter 2

"It's been ten days."

Frustration added a grating whine to Greg Wozniak's voice as he glanced around the small group of scientists, researchers, and intelligence analysts crowded into the oceanographic station's mess.

Several day's growth fuzzed the cheeks of the men. Red rimmed their lids and traced fine lines through the whites of their eyes. Shoulders slumped under layers of wool shirts and thermal underwear.

They were all tired, all showing signs of sleep deprivation and disappointment. The initial burst of excitement that had sustained them through days and nights of constant experimentation and vigilance had seeped away.

"We brought Stone's body temperature back to normal range almost a week ago," Wozniak reminded the group unnecessarily. Shoving his coffee mug aside, he pleaded his case for the third time in as many hours. "We've pumped every possible combination of drugs through the Iceman's veins."

"He has a name," Diana put in coolly.

Ten days of constant contact with the short, rotound cyro-geneticist hadn't improved her opinion of him. Wozniak shrugged and picked up the threads of his argument.

"We can't use the paddles on Stone's heart many more times or we'll completely destroy the muscle. I think it's time to officially declare him dead and let me get on with the cloning process."

Across the table from Diana, Dr. Irwin Goode wrapped thin hands around his mug. Liver spots darkened his fragile skin. His fingers trembled. She'd heard the Nobel Prize winner speak at a convention some years ago and was saddened to see how much the brilliant scientist had aged. If his body had succumbed to the march of time, however, his mind still functioned with razor-edged sharpness.

"Major Stone's brain showed evidence of low level activity after the first shock," the silver-haired Goode reminded his younger colleague calmly.

"Not enough to restart his biorhythms."

"But enough to allow an early determination that

he's not completely brain dead. As you're well aware, the law as currently written doesn't allow cloning live human subjects without their consent.''

''I know!'' Wozniak groused. ''It's just my luck Stone doesn't have any close relatives left alive to authorize the procedure.''

With some effort, Diana bit back a sarcastic comment on his warm, caring humanity.

''We agreed on one more attempt,'' Goode reminded him. ''If the current combination of proteins and acids we're pumping into him don't produce cell activity, we'll reevaluate the protocol.''

''Pull the plug, you mean,'' Diana muttered.

Behind the lens of his rimless glasses, Dr. Goode's eyes held a look of mild reproof. ''I mean we'll reevaluate the protocol.''

She bit her lip, embarrassed by her unprofessional remark. After ten days of intense, around-the-clock trial and error, they were all on edge. And just about out of options.

In her heart of hearts, Diana didn't hold out any more hope of reviving Stone than the others. Yet every time she touched his now warm skin or peered through a microscope at tissue samples to search for signs of protein regeneration, she seemed to lose a little more of her scientific objectivity.

In ten days, Major Charles Stone had become a personal challenge to her, almost a quest. Her years of study, her countless hours of research, all seemed to have led her to this remote, isolated Arctic station.

To him.

Metal chair legs scraped as Diana shoved away from the rickety table. She wasn't ready to give up on the pilot yet. She couldn't. With a nod to her colleagues, she left the small, boxlike room that served as mess hall, card room and conference center.

The recovery team's arrival had severely crowded the already cramped station. To make room for the extra supplies and equipment, the obliging oceanographers had shoved their computers against walls and moved their acoustical sounding devices into the long, snakelike tunnel that connected the collapsible sheds.

Generators hummed as Diana picked her way past stacked boxes and various pieces of gear. The hot air pumped through the double walls kept the temperature inside the station at a toasty sixty-five degrees, so the occupants didn't have to pile on too many layers. Boots, snug leggings and a wool plaid shirt worn open over thermal silk long johns provided Diana with sufficient warmth and a measure of mobility.

Before entering the storage shed where Major Stone lay suspended between life and death, she ducked into the cramped side room the recovery team had converted into a lab. She'd already checked the latest cell samples once this morning but wanted another look.

Hooking a stool with her heel, she dragged it closer to the long, flat counter filled with racks of test tubes and culture dishes. As Dr. Goode had as much as admitted, they were down to their last hope. They'd tried every possible protein and nucleic acid combination within the range of Major Stone's molecular sequencing. If this combination didn't work, if the protein and nucleic acid didn't bind…

Flicking the switch on a laser scanning microscope, Diana slipped a slide with the latest sample under the lens. The air force had spared no cost to lease and ship in the powerful scope Dr. Goode had requested. It was one of only three in use anywhere in the world outside heavily funded and usually guarded research facilities. While Diana squinted at the hugely magnified cells, the microscope's computers whirred through the two hundred thousand plus known protein sequences to verify the sample's profile.

Mere seconds later, the screen blinked a complex code. With a click of the mouse, Diana sent the code to the computer's built-in chart function.

"Damn!"

The line charting this combination remained flat and straight. Major Stone's protein profile hadn't changed by so much as a gnome.

Swallowing a sharp stab of disappointment, she removed the slide and started to push away from the counter. Only then did she notice the faint, almost indiscernible bluish tint at the edge of the sample.

Her breath caught. Snapping the slide back under the lens, she refocused the dual eyepieces at the edge of the slide.

There it was! A complex protein strand that had bonded with traces of nucleic acid! Unless the sample had become contaminated, the bonding was new. So why did the computer spit out the same, dead profile?

Frowning, she reset the computer and ran the entire sequence again. When the identical code came up, she swore softly.

"That can't be right."

Her first instinct was to consult Dr. Goode. Her second, to jab down on the stem of the functional black chronometer strapped to her right wrist.

Before Diana had left D.C., OMEGA's chief of communications had outfitted her with a special transceiver designed to resist the extreme Arctic cold. The device looked like an ordinary twenty-dollar watch, the kind you could buy at any Wal-Mart. As Mackenzie Blair had demonstrated, however, this particular watch contained a hermetically sealed transciever that could send and receive signals from a highly classified defense satellite with bell-ringing clarity.

One quick jab on the stem activated the system and established an instant link.

"Control, this is Artemis. Do you read me?"

Mackenzie's cheerful reply came through a second later. "I've got you, Artemis. Go ahead."

"I need you to access the PIR-PSD through OMEGA's computers."

"Repeat, please."

"The Protein Information Resource-Protein Sequence Database."

"Ooooh-kay."

"It's the largest protein database in the world. Just type PIR-PSD into the computer and you'll go right to it. Tell me when you pull up the home screen."

Chewing on her lower lip, Diana waited for OMEGA's chief of communications to plug into the international information source.

"I'm there," Mackenzie announced a few seconds later.

"I'm going to feed you a long string of numbers. Type them in exactly as I give them to you, then hit the button that says request profile."

"Fire when ready, Artemis."

With meticulous care, Diana read the long series of numbers from the current sample. Mackenzie repeated each digit as she entered it into the computer.

While the PIR-PSD digested the information, Diana's heart thumped painfully. Had the astronomically expensive electron microscope given erroneous readings? Would they have to start over, repeat the thousands of sequences within Major Stone's profile range? Could they keep his organs functioning long enough to…

"I'm getting some kind of a code here."

"Read it to me. Slowly!"

Diana typed the code Mackenzie fed her into the microscope's computer and switched to the chart function. Instantly, the flat line shot upward.

"Ohmigod!"

"Something wrong, Artemis?"

"No! Something's right! Very right!"

Here they'd been within hours of pulling the plug on Major Charles Stone, and his protein had already begun to regenerate. If this chart was anywhere near correct, he'd almost reached sufficient levels to sustain life.

Trembling with excitement, Diana advised Mackenzie she'd report back later and slid off the stool. She should notify Goode and Wozniak and the others, have them verify the anomaly. She would, as soon as she checked on the major.

He lay stretched out on the metal table, atop a computer-controlled aqueous gel mattress to cushion his body and vary his position at timed intervals. He was still naked, although the team had draped a folded sheet over his midsection. Video cameras mounted on tripods observed him from four different angles. IVs snaked from his arm, heart monitor leads from his chest. Electrodes measured the almost imperceptible brain activity that had so excited the team at first. A whole wall of monitors recorded both visual and digital data.

Her heart still pumping pure adrenaline from the chart reading, Diana stepped to the table. Major Stone lay supine, broad shouldered, superbly muscled. Fine brown hair arrowed down his chest, whorled around his navel, and disappeared beneath the folded sheet. The same tobacco brown hair lightly fuzzed his arms and legs. His buzz cut was a darker shade, and right out of the fifties.

As a biologist, Diana appreciated beauty in all life forms. Stone wasn't handsome in a classical sense, she decided. His features were too rugged, his jaw too square and blunt. She had to admit, though, his raw masculinity shot her scientific detachment all to hell. That, and the fact that she had absorbed so many details of his life by now that there was no way she could view him objectively.

According to the extensive background dossier Mackenzie had compiled, Charlie Stone had lost his parents during the Depression and was raised by an aunt. He'd worked at a variety of odd jobs while in high school, but still managed to letter in baseball and football. From the many comments in his high school yearbook, he'd won as many cheerleaders' hearts as he had games.

When World War II broke out, he lied about his age to enlist in the Army Air Corps aviation cadets. He'd flown P-51 Mustangs in Europe, and F-86 Sabre jets six years later in Korea. He'd been engaged for a brief period to an army nurse, but the affair fizzled when she mustered out of the army and went home. Stone had then been selected for test pilot school and moved to Edwards Air Force Base, California, where he flew with the likes of Chuck Yeager and future astronaut Deke Slayton.

He was from the old school. Tough. Tested. The kind of brash, fearless flier who pushed himself and the aircraft he tested to the edge of the envelope. He'd racked up hundreds of hours in various experimental airframes when the CIA had ''requested'' him from the air force to help shake out the bugs on the supersecret U-2. A little more than a year later, he'd dropped out of the sky.

''I wonder what you'll think of your world if…*when* you wake up.''

She laid her hand on his arm, comparing the feel of his skin to the temperature displayed on the monitors. Despite the chill air inside the makeshift laboratory, he was warm to the touch.

''It's not the same world it was in 1956,'' she said, willing him to hear her voice, hoping he'd respond to the stimulus of human contact. ''From what I've read about the Cold War era, I think you'll find it's better. Then again, maybe we haven't come as far as we like to think we have.''

She stroked his arm gently, dredging up images from his time. Eisenhower facing off with Kruschev. Sputnik. Polio victims imprisoned in huge iron lungs. *I Love Lucy* and *Howdy Doody* in grainy black and white. Chrome-laden Cadillacs with sharklike fins. Or did all that chrome come later?

She'd have to pull up the interactive time capsule Mackenzie had compiled. The gee-whiz program provided visuals and audio on everything from popular foods of the fifties to Hit Parade favorites crooned by the likes of Patti Page and Frankie Laine.

''We've conquered polio,'' she told him, ''but Lucy and Ricky still reign supreme on late-night TV. You can catch them just about… Yikes!''

She jumped back, almost choking in surprise as the arm she'd been stroking jerked straight up.

Disbelieving, Diana gaped at the upraised limb. Was it just a reflex? A response to the stimulus of her touch?

Her heart pounding, she dragged her astonished gaze from his arm to his face and nearly jumped again. His eyelids twitched. She was sure they'd twitched.

''Major Stone!'' Her voice spiraled to an excited squeak. ''Can you hear me?''

His forehead creased in a frown.

''Major Stone!'' Her pulse hammered so hard and fast she could scarcely breathe. ''Open your eyes.''

Deep grooves bracketed his mouth. The muscles of his neck corded, making Diana's own throat ache painfully. From the corner of one eye, she saw the bank of monitors light up like a Christmas tree. A shrill beep sounded, stretched into warning buzz. Another alarm pinged. Within seconds, a whole chorus was chirping away.

The alarms brought one of the research techs rushing through the door behind her. ''What's going on?''

''He's waking up!'' Diana threw over her shoulder. ''Get Dr. Goode. Immediately.''

She whipped back around and felt every ounce of oxygen leave her lungs.

He'd opened his eyes! Wild confusion filled their blue depths.

''It's all right.'' Reining in her galloping excitement, she infused her voice with deliberate, soothing calm. ''You're safe. You're at the U.S. Arctic Oceanographic station.''

His eyes narrowed, dissected her face, her red-and-brown plaid shirt, her jeans. When he brought his gaze back to hers, his throat worked. A sound halfway between a groan and a croak escaped.

''Don't try to talk yet.''

He jerked his arm again and grabbed a fistful of her shirt. Astonished by his strength, she let him drag her down until their faces were only inches apart. With an effort that was painful to watch, he swallowed and tried again. Finally, he forced out a single syllable.

"Who…?"

"Who am I? My name is Diana Remington. Dr. Diana Remington."

She heard the sound of running footsteps behind her. Greg Wozniak barreled through the door. Excitement and his dash down the hall had turned his chubby face brick red.

"Is it true? Is he waking up?"

"See for yourself."

Diana started to edge aside. The hold on her shirt kept her tethered to the table as Major Stone's gaze shifted to her colleague.

"I… I don't believe it!" Wozniak breathed, almost as inarticulate as their subject. "How…? When…?"

Diana waited until a huffing Dr. Goode had joined them to relate the astounding sequence of events.

"It happened so fast. Without warning. I was in here checking his vitals when his arm jerked. A few seconds later, his eyes opened."

Goode's glance was riveted on Stone. Little of the excitement Diana and Greg Wozniak were feeling showed on his wrinkled face.

"I don't understand it. The sequence profiles

showed no indication that his protein was beginning to regenerate.''

As much as Diana wanted to share the results of the test she'd had Mackenzie run using OMEGA's computers, she couldn't break her cover. ''The microscope must have been giving us faulty readings.''

''Impossible,'' Goode stated emphatically. ''I calibrated it myself.''

''Well, one of the solutions we fed him obviously worked.'' Still pinned against the table by Stone's grip on her shirt, Diana made the introductions. ''Major Stone, this is Dr. Irwin Goode, a Nobel Prize winner in bionetics. He worked with the U-2 spy plane program years ago. And this is Dr. Greg Wozniak, who...''

She broke off, gasping, as Stone's biceps flexed again. With a sharp tug, he yanked her down. She ended up sprawled across his body, with one hand planted square on his naked chest, the other scrabbling for a grip on the metal table. Ice blue eyes lasered into hers.

''Not...spy,'' he rasped with savage intensity. ''Wea...ther flight.''

Oh, Lord! In her excitement, she'd forgotten that the U-2 program was so highly classified during Major Stone's time that not even Congress knew about the intelligence gathering flights over the Soviet Union. It had been a CIA show from start to finish, back in the days when the agency called all the shots without any pesky laws or Congressional oversight to curb their operations.

From the information Mackenzie had put together on the U-2 program, the operation was classic CIA. The pilots stripped down to the skin before climbing into their flight suits. They carried no personal items, wore no identifying insignia or rank. Even their aircraft was unmarked. If forced down over enemy territory, they'd been instructed to deny any attempt at intelligence gathering and admit only to collecting weather data.

Which is exactly what Major Stone was doing now.

"It's okay," she said, trying to lever up a few inches. "The U-2 program is no longer classified."

He didn't let go. If anything, his scowl grew even fiercer.

Diana's OMEGA training had included brutal and highly effective techniques for breaking just about any hold, but she figured smashing Stone's wrist bones against the edge of the metal table wouldn't exactly win his confidence.

"It's okay," she repeated, ignoring the fact that her breasts flattened against his chest and her mouth hovered only inches from his. "We're on your side."

His jaw worked. "Wea-ther flight."

Oh boy! He obviously intended to stick to his oath to keep all aspects of his mission secret.

Admiration for his courage gripped Diana. He had to be confused, disoriented. Had to be wondering how in the world he'd arrived at a remote oceanographic station. Yet he wasn't about to admit to a thing except his cover story.

"You can trust us," she said softly. "We know you're Major Charles Stone, United States Air Force. We know you were detailed to the CIA in early 1955 to test and put into operation a new, single-seat, high-altitude reconnaissance aircraft. We also know you were flying that aircraft when it disappeared from radar at 2235 hours on November 2, 1956. What we don't know is *why* it went down, but we're hoping you'll tell us that."

He stared at her, his features taut and grim. After what seemed like a lifetime, his grip on her shirt loosened. She eased up a few inches.

She didn't say anything for several moments, wanting to give him time to digest what he'd heard so far before she dropped the bomb about his forty-five year snooze. She looked to her colleagues, then back at Stone, only to discover that his glance had locked on something just over her shoulder.

"What...the...hell?"

The harsh, rasping exclamation ripped from deep in his throat. Diana took a quick look behind her, saw the digital clock mounted on the wall. The time, day, month, and year flashed in iridescent green.

Dragging in a deep breath, she faced the Iceman again.

"Yes," she said slowly and clearly. "That's the correct date."

Chapter 3

It was a plot! A crazy Commie scheme to confuse him. Disorient him. Make him spill his guts. It couldn't be anything else!

Desperately, Charlie tried to shatter the ice that seemed to have crystallized inside his brain. Images shimmered against the white haze in his mind. Sounds came and went. Sharp cracks. Long groans. Like icebergs crying when they broke free of a glacier. With each image, each sound, fear rose in black, billowing waves.

Thrusting it back with a silent snarl, Charlie reached into the void and grabbed onto the fragments he could remember with both hands. He'd taken off from his base in Turkey. Flown a routine mission. Just entered Soviet airspace when…when all hell broke loose. He'd jerked the stick, had tried desperately to bring his plane around and escape Soviet airspace before he bailed out.

The fragments shifted, grew clearer. He remembered the suffocating lack of oxygen, recalled fumbling for the ejection handle. And the cold. God, the cold! It tore at his eyeballs, sliced into his skin. Then the bone-wrenching jolt of his parachute. After that, nothing.

He must have come down in Siberia. Or splashed into the Bering Sea and been fished out by seal hunters or fishermen. They'd no doubt turned him over to the Soviet authorities. Nothing else could explain the absurd tale the woman still sprawled across his chest was concocting.

As if she'd crawled right into his skull and had decoded his every thought, she confirmed his point of impact. "All indications are that you went down in the Arctic Ocean, Major Stone."

He was so shaken by her uncanny ability to read his mind, he barely grasped the incredible story she spun for him.

"Immersion in the freezing Arctic water reduced the need for oxygen in your brain at the same rate your circulation slowed. In effect, you went into a state of deep, permanent hibernation. Your pressure suit protected your body from decomposition."

Sympathy glimmered in the green eyes so close

to his own, but Charlie refused to acknowledge it, just as his scrambling mind flatly refuted the soft statement that followed.

''You've been lost in the ice for forty-five years.''

She was good. Damned good. She looked so sincere, sounded so American! Charlie's lip curled.

''Helluva...story, blon...die,'' he rasped, his throat raw and aching. ''Too bad...I'm not buying it.''

''It's true.''

''Yeah, and...I'm Joe...DiMaggio.''

The Commies knew just how to wring a man's head inside out. Charlie had flown during the Korea War. He'd lost buddies, had heard tales about the POWs who'd disappeared into China. Only now, three years after the war had finally ended, was the truth beginning to seep out.

The Soviet masters of both North Korea and China had perfected a technique the CIA labeled brainwashing. According to highly classified reports, they'd programmed American POWs to betray their country, burying the traitorous impulse so deep in their psyche that no one, even the POWs themselves, knew it existed.

The CIA had proof, had shown Charlie and his fellow U-2 pilots the case file of a lieutenant who'd returned home to lead a quiet, ordinary life as a Frigidaire salesman until something or someone had triggered him. Without warning, the former officer had walked off the job, retrieved his hunting rifle, and calmly put a bullet through the powerful senator who was making a whistle stop campaign appearance in town that afternoon. To this day, the lieutenant had no idea why he'd killed the charismatic presidential candidate.

Charlie wasn't about to let this green-eyed blonde play with his head.

"I know it's hard to believe, Major Stone," she was saying calmly, "but I'm telling you the truth. You're at an American oceanographic station one hundred and eighty miles north of Point Barrow, Alaska. And the date is really June 2002."

The woman—what had she called herself? Remington. *Dr.* Remington—pushed against his chest with the flat of her palm.

"If you'll let me up, perhaps my colleagues and I can convince you."

Charlie wasn't about to admit he didn't have the strength to hold her if she fought him. He was shaking like a kitten, so weak the mere act of uncurling his fist took every ounce of strength he possessed. Sweat popped out on his skin, chilling him instantly. Only then did he realize he was stretched out flat on a table, as naked as a skinned coon. Tubes and wires snaked from his arms, legs and chest.

His gaze narrowing, he followed the tangled umbilical cords to the bank of equipment they sprouted from. Another wave of shivers rippled along the surface of his skin. As one of the first test pilots selected for the U-2 high altitude program, Charlie had been poked and prodded and subjected to just about every experiment known to man. Yet he'd never seen equipment like this.

Setting his jaw, he reached across his chest. With one vicious tug, he ripped the IV from his arm. Drops of blood and intravenous solution sprayed around the room.

"Hey!" The short, balding man beside blondie jumped back. "Careful with those bodily fluids! They're as dangerous as a machine gun!"

Charlie's throat closed. What the hell had they pumped into him?

The woman—Remington—shot her companion a look of disgust. "If you're worried about AIDS, Greg, the first case wasn't documented until 1981, twenty-five years after Major Stone dropped out of the sky."

The man reddened, but kept his distance. "Who knows what he picked up in the ice? There has to be some reason for the anomaly in his protein regeneration."

None of what they were saying made the least sense to Charlie, but one thought surfaced crystal clear through his swirling confusion. No one was going to stick anything else in him—or take any further readings—until he figured out what the hell was happening here. Setting his jaw, he swung his legs to the side of the table and pushed himself up.

His head buzzed. The ring of faces around him blurred. Gritting his teeth, Charlie blinked to clear the swirling haze and proceeded to yank off every telemetry lead.

"Major Stone!"

"Don't hurt yourself!"

"Careful with the equipment."

His fierce glare silenced the instant chorus. Chest heaving, Charlie gripped the metal table with both hands. His breath rasped on the cold air, the only sound in the lab until the blonde broke the tension.

"Why don't we make you more comfortable? I believe some clothes would be in order, and a move to the living quarters. Is that agreeable to you, Major?"

Stone's gaze roamed the makeshift lab, taking in the monitors and cameras, before locking with hers again. A curt nod signaled his acquiescence.

To the fierce disappointment of everyone on recovery team, Diana included, Major Stone lived up to his name and made like a rock. Once installed in a hastily cleared bunk room and outfitted in borrowed clothing, he crossed his arms and refused to answer questions or respond to the team's revelations. Nor was he ready to accept that he'd awakened in the second millennium *A.D.*

The team tried their best to convince him, presenting printed material, digitized images and TV shows beamed in by satellite over the station's system. The major's eyes narrowed to slits as he stared at the flickering images, but he kept all thoughts to himself.

At one point, Diana thought they'd finally gotten through to him, but Dr. Wozniak's excited explanation of the cloning process and impassioned request for a DNA sample produced another severe case of lockjaw.

No one, he declared ominously, was going to produce a test tube duplicate while he was able to prevent it.

"It was bad enough when he thought we were trying to worm information on the U-2 program out of him," Diana reported to OMEGA's new chief some hours later. "After we sprang the fact that he's been on ice for more than four decades, he shut down completely. My guess is he thinks we're playing mind games with him in an effort to get him to talk."

"So he hasn't said anything about his aircraft or what happened to it?"

"Roger that, Lightning."

"His mental condition sounds pretty stable. How's his overall physical condition?"

"Incredible. Absolutely incredible."

If Nick noticed the husky note in her voice, he

chose not to comment on it. "Do you still have him under close observation?"

"In a manner of speaking. We've moved him into living quarters and posted a research tech outside his door...just in case he decides to depart the station."

"Well, keep me advised on his progress."

"Will do, Lighting."

She started to sign off, hesitated. "Did you dig anything up on Greg Wozniak?"

"Not yet. We're still looking into his financial holdings. They're nothing if not diversified. In addition to his lucrative research grants, he owns a chain of sperm banks and a piece of several companies that manufacture cyrogenic equipment. But his real money appears to come from wealthy clients who pay him six figures or more to freeze a part of themselves for future cloning."

"Have any of those clients availed themselves of his service?"

"None that we're aware of."

"So Stone would have really been a feather in Wozniak's cap professionally, as well as a walking advertisement for his business. No wonder he was so eager for the recovery team to declare the major legally dead."

"Eager enough to somehow falsify the protein profiles?"

Suspicion was an ugly little worm, one every undercover agent learned to live with. This particular worm had been turning and twisting in Diana's mind since she'd discovered the faulty readings.

"I don't know."

"Keep an eye on him," Nick advised. "In the meantime, we'll dig deeper."

"Roger that."

Signing off, she arched her back and hooked her hands behind her neck to relieve the kinks.

Lord, she was tired! Even without the strain of the recovery operation, she would have found it difficult to sleep in the bright, perpetual haze of an Arctic summer. After ten days, her internal clock was still struggling to adjust. She knew she wouldn't get much more rest tonight than she had the previous nights. Charlie Stone would invade her sleep, just as he'd dominated her waking hours.

Wondering what he was doing right now, she tugged off her boots. Was he studying the magazines they'd left in his room? Flipping through the switches on the satellite-fed TV? Prowling his eight-by-eight room?

She had her answer not two minutes later.

She had just bent over a stainless steel sink to splash her face with bottled water when the snick of a door opening brought her twisting around. Despite her dripping lashes, she recognized the major's wide-shouldered, narrow-hipped form instantly.

"Major Stone!"

She bobbed upright, blinking the water from her eyes. He looked so different in borrowed tan work pants and an ill-fitting blue shirt that stretched at the shoulder seams. His boots were his own, she noted in a quick sweep, the same high-topped brown lace-ups the team had studied and analyzed as part of the recovery effort.

"How did you…?"

"How did I escape my guard?"

His voice was still rough, still raspy, but there was no mistaking the lethal edge to it.

"He wasn't a guard."

"You could have fooled me."

He crossed the room in two swift strides, backing Diana against the wall beside the sink.

"He's just a research technician," she said as calmly as she could with his blue eyes blazing down at her. "There to help you if you wanted anything. You didn't hurt him, did you?"

"He won't show any bruises, if that's what you're worried about."

His balled fists and threatening stance didn't intimidate her. She could take him down if she had to. What bothered the hell out of her was the fact that his proximity was causing every nerve in her body to snap with an almost electrical intensity.

"What do you want?" she asked coolly.

"The truth. Who are you?"

"I told you. My name is Diana Remington. I flew

up here, along with Drs. Goode and Wozniak and the others, when your body was recovered from…''

''Don't hand me that crap about being buried in the ice for forty-five years again!''

''It's true.''

His reply was short and decidedly scatological.

''What will it take to convince you?'' she asked. ''How many documents or videos do you need?''

''Documents can be faked. So can those whiz-bang movies you showed me.''

''Why in the world would we go to so much trouble?''

''You tell me, blondie.''

Angling her chin, she met his belligerence head on. ''I'm not a Communist propagandist trying to get into your skull and play mind games. The Cold War is over. We won. The Wall came tumbling down.''

''What wall?''

Too late, she remembered that the ultimate symbol of the Cold War, the Berlin Wall, hadn't been erected until years after Stone went into the ice.

''Never mind. All that matters right now is that the U.S. halted top-secret U-2 overflights of Russia in 1960, right after Francis Gary Powers bailed out. You don't have to guard your identity or that of your unit with your life. They're history. *You're* history,'' she added more gently.

A muscle worked in the side of his jaw. "What brought Gary's plane down?"

"A surface to air missile."

"Bull! The Dragon Lady flies too high and too fast for Soviet SAMs to reach her."

"Maybe in your time, but by 1960, the Soviets had significantly improved their missile capability. So had the U.S., for that matter."

"How do I know you're telling the truth?"

"You can pull up information about Powers's trial on any computer. Or look him up in the encyclopedia," she added, remembering just in time Stone's reaction to the station's desktop PCs.

In his day, computers were gargantuan monsters that filled an entire room. He'd regarded the smaller, exponentially faster versions of the old vacuum tube models with both suspicion and an awe he'd tried his damndest to disguise.

"Powers served two years in a Soviet prison before being exchanged," Diana said briskly. "I think he wrote a book about his experiences before he died in a helicopter crash in the seventies."

For an instant, just an instant, she glimpsed a desolation as bleak as the vast Arctic emptiness in his face. Stone had lost both parents while he was still a kid. With no brothers or sisters, he'd made the military his family, his fellow aviators his kin. Now most of them would now be gone, too.

Diana could only imagine what it would be like

to wake up and find yourself alone in an alien world, without friends or familiar landmarks. Steeling herself, she fought the urge to lift a hand and stroke his cheek. He hadn't asked for comfort or condolences, and probably wouldn't appreciate either.

"Why don't we sit down, Major Stone?"

She took a single step, only to come up short as two palms slapped the wall beside her head. His arms caged her. His body formed a solid, immovable wall.

"I want a few more answers first."

"All right. But just so you know, this type of primitive, caveman behavior went the way of the poodle skirt and the Studebaker."

It took him a moment to process her acidic comment. When the meaning registered, a look of almost comical dismay crossed his face.

"Are you saying my Golden Hawk is obsolete?"

"It is if it was produced by Studebaker."

"Well, hell! I've only made two payments on that baby."

With each passing moment, Diana felt less like her mythical incarnation of a huntress and more like the legendary Cassandra, the deliverer of doom and evil tidings. Not only had she broken the news his buddy had died, but now she'd hit him in one of an American male's most vulnerable spots...his car.

She gave him a moment or two to mourn before

prodding gently. "What else did you want to ask me?"

Shaking off his gloom, he pinned her with a hard look. "What's your connection to Irwin Goode?"

Surprised, she answered truthfully. "I suppose you could say we're colleagues, although that would be stretching matters considerably. Actually, he's way out of my league. He won a Nobel Prize for his early work in bionetics. Even today, his pioneering study of the effects of certain toxic agents on red blood cells is standard college-level textbook reading."

Stone remained silent for so long Diana had to fight the urge to fidget. He was too close and too... Too male. Nothing at all like Allen.

The thought popped into her head before she could stop it. She flushed, feeling disloyal to her steady date of some months and more than a little irritated by Stone's sledgehammer impact on her senses.

"Did you know Dr. Goode back when you were flying the U-2?" she asked.

He opened his mouth, snapped it shut again. Evidently he still wasn't ready to admit he actually flew the supersecret spy plane. With a sigh, Diana tried to move away again.

"I'm not done with you, blondie."

"I'll tell you what," she said with a determined

smile. "If you refrain from calling me blondie, I'll refrain from tossing you flat on your back."

A speculative gleam entered his eyes. "Do you think you can?"

"I know it, pal."

For a moment he looked as though he intended to put the matter to a test. His gaze made a slow slide from her face to her throat, then lingered in the vicinity of her breasts. To Diana's surprise and considerable annoyance, her nipples tingled under her silk long johns, and the queerest sensation gripped her belly.

Oh, for heaven's sake!

In today's parlance, Stone certainly qualified as a world class hottie. But as much as Diana might admire his sheer animal magnetism, muscle alone had never particularly turned her on. Unlike the athletic, popular Stone, she'd been the serious, studious type in high school. She'd come out of her shell a bit in college, and discarded it completely when Maggie Sinclair recruited her to work for OMEGA. Yet she'd always found that brains, not brawn worked better when it came to wiggling out of the most desperate situations.

And, she reminded herself sternly, brains, not brawn, had attracted her to Allen McDermott. They enjoyed a comfortable, mutually satisfying relationship, one that stemmed as much from their similar tastes and shared professional interests as from any physical need.

But she'd never felt a need quite like this one, a nasty little voice in her head whispered.

Not with Allen.

Not with anyone.

Ruthlessly, Diana suppressed the insidious urge to rise up on tiptoe and give Charlie Stone his first kiss in more than forty-five years. She was here to do a job, one that demanded all her concentration. She'd be no use to OMEGA or to the major if she didn't maintain a level of detachment.

"If you've finished with your questions," she said coolly, "I have a few I'd like to ask."

His arms dropped to his sides, and a steel mask descended over his face with an almost audible clank. "I don't trust you enough to give you any answers."

"Well, that's honest. Let me know when you change your mind, will you?"

"Yeah," he replied, heading for the door. "I will."

Charlie made it out the door with his shoulders squared and his back straight, but his insides felt as though he'd just gone ten rounds with heavyweight champ Rocky Marciano.

Everything he'd seen since he opened his eyes hit him like a hard, bruising right to the gut. Everything he'd heard had rocked him back on his heels. Sheer willpower alone had kept him from grabbing his so-called rescuers by the throat and choking the truth out of them.

He didn't want to believe them! Christ, just the thought that he'd been on ice for the past forty-five years made his stomach cramp.

He braced himself against a packing crate, unable to stop the shakes, unable to blank out the terrifying memory of his plane nosediving straight down. Desperately, he tried to pierce the blackness that had claimed him mere seconds later. Had he come down inside Russia? Was this all an elaborate KGB scheme to get him to talk?

No. Even the KGB couldn't cook up something this fantastic.

Slowly, Charlie's vision cleared. The disbelief he'd so stubbornly clung to these past hours was fast giving way to grudging acceptance. He wasn't ready to admit it. Not yet, anyway. Until he found out what the hell had happened to his aircraft and why his life support system had failed, he wasn't about to admit to anything.

Particularly not to blondie.

Man, oh man! They sure didn't build biologists like her where he came from. If she *was* a biologist. None of the scientists he'd ever worked with came equipped with luminous green cat's eyes and a tumble of silver-gilt hair, not to mention those long legs displayed so temptingly in her curve-hugging pants. Those pants certainly left little to the imagination, and his worked overtime until a muffled thump from inside his room broke into his thoughts. With a grunt, he entered the room and opened the metal locker.

The young research tech hopped out, glaring at Charlie over the tape sealing his mouth. More tape bound his wrists and ankles.

"Sorry, kid."

Freed of his bonds, the technician stomped out. A moment later, Charlie heard him hammering on a door farther down the corridor. In an angry voice, he recounted the details of his incarceration.

Thoughtfully, Charlie recrossed the small room and flipped the latch on his own door. Any determined six-year-old could kick through the flimsy panel, but at least the noise would provide some warning. That done, he dug into the pile of flight gear he'd retrieved from the lab before paying his unannounced visit to the woman next door.

His fingers stroked the white helmet that screwed onto the collar of his flight suit, lingering on the metal opening where his oxygen tube had connected. The rubberized rings sealing the opening had crumbled away, but the helmet itself had gone into the sea intact. So had Charlie's leather belt with its holstered .45 automatic and sheathed knife.

Sliding the Colt from its leather nest, he took it

apart and checked every component. It was in excellent condition, all things considered. Thoughtfully, he reassembled the weapon, snapped the magazine in place, and chambered a round.

As he'd told blondie, he wasn't ready to trust her...or anyone else in her world.

Chapter 4

Diana soon discovered that winning Major Stone's trust had become a game, one played by two skilled opponents who made up the rules as they went along. The contest began the very next morning when he showed up at the mess hall. The research tech detailed to watch him trailed at his heels, wary and still more than a little disgruntled after his incarceration in the metal wall locker.

Diana was already at the mess, nursing her first cup of coffee and relating the essence of her conversation with the major the previous evening to the other members of the recovery team. She broke off as the subject under discussion appeared at the entrance to the mess.

All eyes turned to the new arrival. Stone had been fed the station's regular menu—such as it was!—since he'd ripped out his IV yesterday, but this was the first time he'd ventured into the common area itself.

Clearing her throat, Diana broke the startled silence. "Good morning, Major Stone."

He stood on the threshold, surveying the motley crew. The oceanographers had racked up months of station duty, with limited bathing facilities and out-of-whack internal body clocks. As a result, most of them sported scraggly beards, bags under their eyes and layers of mismatched clothing. The recovery team had only been on station eleven days now, but looked almost as bad.

Wishing she'd taken time to do more than splash her face, drag a comb through her hair and throw a baggy brown sweater over her leggings and long johns, Diana scooted her chair over a few inches.

"Why don't you come in and join us?"

He claimed the seat next to hers and listened intently while she introduced the men he hadn't met yet, including the oceanographer who'd first spotted him.

"You about gave me a heart attack," the scientist admitted wryly. "I don't think I'm ever going to forget the sight of you staring back at me through the ice."

"Thanks for digging me out."

He said the words slowly, as if he still wasn't entirely sure he was grateful for being rescued.

"Yeah, well, it's gotta be tough, what you're going through. I'm just glad the recovery team managed to, uh, defrost you."

"So am I." His glance made a circuit of the table, lingering briefly on Greg Wozniak and Irwin Goode before focusing on Diana. "I think."

With a bland smile, she reached behind her and poured a cup of the thick black sludge that the station crew loosely defined as coffee.

"Here," she said, sliding him the mug. "This is guaranteed to warm up any unthawed parts."

He accepted the cup and downed a quick swallow. The bright yellow box on the table snagged his attention.

"What's in that?"

"Breakfast."

While various crew members looked on, Stone slid a cellophane-wrapped frozen waffle from the box. He turned it over and over, examining its rocklike consistency.

"They're not bad," Diana assured him. "Want to try one?"

He glanced at the plates of the other diners, where the remains of their breakfast swam in pools of rich, dark syrup.

"All right, I'm game."

He held out the cellophane pack, obviously expecting her to cook the contents for him. She lifted her mug and treated herself to a leisurely swallow.

"There's a toaster right behind you. Just take the waffle out of the wrapping and pop it in."

He got the message. The cellophane crackled under his fingers as he eyed her curiously. "Are you trying to tell me women don't cook where you come from?"

When she came from was what he meant, as everyone at the table silently acknowledged. The major still wasn't ready to admit the truth.

"Popping a waffle into a toaster hardly qualifies as cooking," she replied breezily, "but you'll find men and women share most household tasks today."

From the furtive glances some of the other males at the table exchanged, it appeared they wouldn't mind a return to the fifties, or at least television's version of it. They'd probably love to have a June Cleaver look-alike in pearls, high heels and flawless makeup vacuuming the house and preparing dinner for Beaver, Wally and Dad.

Dream on, boys!

At least she'd set Charlie Stone's feet on the right path for acclimation to his brave new world. She was savoring her small victory over the forces of evil when a sudden doubt hit her. Biting down on her lower lip, she watched Charlie examine the chrome toaster. When the heck had that particular appliance been invented, anyway?

"Do know how to operate it? You just put the waffle in and…"

"Push down on the lever," he finished dryly.

"Good. In that case, we can advance to the microwave. Come on, while your waffles are crisping I'll show you how to nuke bacon."

"Nuke?" He froze half out of his chair. "You have nukes at this station?"

"No," Diana said hastily. "It's just an expression, a term we use nowadays for cooking something in the microwave oven."

It didn't take long for Diana to conclude that acclimating Charlie Stone to the twenty-first century would take considerably more effort than she'd imagined. Not only had he missed out on four decades of technological advancements, his attitude toward women in general and Diana in particular was in serious need of adjustment.

He spent the morning with the recovery team, listening to their theories on how he survived the ice, but volunteering neither information about his mission nor theories of his own. Nor would he agree to provide urine or blood samples for analysis. Greg Wozniak's repeated hard sell of the cloning process made him doubly wary of donating any bodily fluids. Frustrated, the team had no choice but to shut down the on-site recovery effort.

"That's fine with me," the major rasped. "When do I leave?"

"As soon as we can call in a plane to ferry us all out," Dr. Goode said calmly. "We'll fly the team back to the aeromedical research facility at Brooks Air Force Base in San Antonio and continue the tests there."

"No dice. I'm going back to Edwards."

"But..."

"It's my home base. I have..." His face darkened. "I once had friends there. Some of them might still be around."

Dr. Goode took off his rimless glasses and polished them carefully with his shirttail. When he settled them back on the bridge of his nose, his eyes were just as hard as his recalcitrant patient's.

"I'm afraid I can't allow you to set the parameters here, Major Stone. You're a biological and medical miracle. You owe it to science to allow us to study you."

"I guess I don't see it that way, Doc. Not at the moment, anyway. If what you've told me is true—and I'm still not ready to concede that it is—I've lost forty-five years of what would have been my life. I don't plan to spend the next few living under a microscope."

"Just what *do* you plan to do?"

"I'll figure that out when I get back to California."

When Diana repeated the exchange to OMEGA's director later that afternoon, Nick left no doubt as to her role in Charlie Stone's immediate future.

"You'll have to stay with him, Artemis."

"For how long?"

"Until after the president's trip to Russia next month or Stone tells us what happened to his plane, whichever comes first."

Judging by Charlie's stubborn refusal to talk, Diana guessed it would be the former and not the latter.

"Do you really think we can keep him under wraps for another two weeks?" she asked dubiously.

"The recovery team and oceanographic researchers there at the station all understand the need for absolute secrecy. We'll make sure the air force personnel at his home base do, too. Just to be certain, though, I'll have Communications run a transmission screen for possible leaks and handle any necessary damage control at this end. Your job is to keep Major Stone away from the media or some enterprising soul who might try to sell his story to the tabloids."

"Which could be anyone or everyone he talks to," she muttered.

"And they told us this undercover business would be so easy," Lightning replied with a smile in his voice.

"Yeah, right. Okay, you get Comm working those screens and I'll try to convince Major Stone he can't live without me for the next few weeks."

The smile lingered in Nick's eyes as he ended the transmission. Diana was one of their best. Like the goddess she was named for, she'd keep Charlie Stone in her bow sights until she brought him to his knees.

The man didn't have a chance.

Still smiling, he hit the buzzer on his intercom. Elizabeth Wells's cheerful voice answered a second later. "Yes, sir?"

The 'sir' still made Nick blink, but he was fast getting used to it. "Ask Comm to come down, will you?"

"Right away."

Leaning back in the buttery-soft leather chair, he stretched out his legs and shoved his hands in his pockets of his slacks. The slacks were hand-tailored, as were his black silk turtleneck and cashmere sports jacket. Nick preferred more casual styles in his clothes, in his home, in the menus he personally selected for his restaurants. Casual and elegant and very, very expensive.

His smile tipped into a wry grin. If it weren't for

the scars he'd accumulated as a youth, even he would have to search hard under the silk and cashmere to find the remnants of the runty, perpetually hungry pickpocket who'd prowled the alleyways of Cannes.

That was how Mackenzie found him when she breezed in a few moments later—stretched out like a sleek, well-fed lion. His dark gold hair and rust-colored jacket fostered the image, she thought with a dart of grudging admiration.

Hey, it didn't hurt to look! She'd learned that much from her ex, who'd also taught her not to come within touching distance of someone like Nick Jensen.

"You rang?"

Idly, Nick jingled the change in his pocket. He knew about the communications chief's messy divorce. Knew, too, that the raven-haired ex-navy officer had come to work at OMEGA with a chip the size of New Hampshire on her shoulder. A chip that seemed to double in intensity whenever she was in Nick's immediate vicinity. One of these days, he mused, he might just have to knock it off.

"I need you to set up a screen of all wire, optical and radio transmissions made by members of the recovery team the Arctic Oceanographic team, and whoever Major Stone meets with when he returns to Edwards Air Force Base. Artemis will supply a daily list."

"That's going to be some screen!"

"Can you and your people do it?"

Her professional pride scratched, she sent him a look that would have felled a lesser man. "Yes."

"That's all, Comm."

"Aye, aye, skipper!"

Executing a smart about-face, Mackenzie left the lion lazing in his den.

Deciding to waste no time executing her revised orders, Diana went in search of the major. She found him in the cramped cubbyhole that passed for the station's exercise room. He'd decided to use the time until the C-130 arrived regaining his full strength, he informed her. Crossing her arms, she leaned against the wall and watched while his still wary watchdog explained the workings of the ergonomic bike.

"You punch in your age and gender here and set the aerobic level you want to achieve. Then you slip your arm into the cuff and wait for the computer to record your resting heart rate before you start pedaling."

"Does everything in your world come equipped with a computer?"

The research tech thought about it for a moment. "Pretty much."

Shaking his head, Charlie gestured to the universal gym. "What about this? Do you need anything more than muscle power to operate this?"

The thin, pallid tech eyed the complicated network of bars, pulleys and weights dubiously. "I don't think so. I'll have to get one of the oceanographers to check you out on it, though."

Diana pushed away from the wall. "I can show him how it works."

Relieved, the research assistant left the major in her capable hands.

"The equipment is currently positioned for leg presses. In this configuration, it works your quadriceps, gluteus maximus, calves and hamstrings."

Not that Major Stone's needed working.

Sternly banishing the wayward thought, she locked in the weights, slid into the seat and gripped the foam-covered handles mounted on either side.

"The principle is to vary the resistance applied to an entire muscle group through exercise." Grunting, Diana raised the stack of weights and brought it down. "You need to maintain a steady rhythm for maximum musculoskeletal and cardiovascular benefit."

The black weights clacking, she gave him a short demonstration. He observed the process with a quizzical expression.

"What?" she asked.

"Is weight lifting standard training for molecular biologists?"

"Nope. Only for those addicted to hot fudge sundaes."

And for undercover operatives, she added silently. Stone's hair would probably stand on end if he caught a glimpse of the torture OMEGA had put Diana and her fellow agents through under the guise of training.

Then again, maybe it wouldn't. Flying fighters in two wars and subsequently qualifying as a test pilot had probably pegged his endurance meter out at max capacity.

"You can also work your upper body," she told him.

Shrugging out of her baggy sweater, she tossed it over a side support. A quick push shoved the sleeves of her thermal silk long johns up to her elbows. Hopping into the upright chair, she grasped the handlebars.

"In the forward position, you isolate the deltoids and triceps." Puffing a little, she went to a ten-count. "Eight, nine...ten."

With a squeak of the chair she spun around and grasped the handlebars from behind. "In reverse position, you... work...the...shoulders. Six. Seven. Eight. Niiii...ne. Ugggh...ten!"

The iron weights hit with a clatter. Arms hooked over the handlebars, Diana blew a loose strand of hair away from her face. She was puffing in earnest now, and not particularly happy about it.

"Guess I'm a little out of shape."

"Not from where I'm standing."

The gruff reply brought her head up. Her skittering pulse took another jump when she caught the direction of Stone's gaze. It was fixed squarely on her chest.

"When did women stop wearing brassieres?" he got out on a growl. "Not that I'm complaining, you understand. Just asking."

"Some of us never started."

He brought his glance back to hers. "Well, what do you know? Maybe there might be some benefit to skipping a few decades, after all."

"Careful," she warned. "You're treading dangerous political waters here."

"How did politics get into the discussion?"

"There's a whole movement that started back in the seventies called Women's Liberation. It embraces the concepts of equal pay for equal work, shattering glass ceilings and generally throwing off the shackles that have kept women barefoot, pregnant and in the kitchen for so long."

"Cooking being one of those shackles?"

"You catch on quickly."

"Maybe. Tell me more about this so-called movement."

A fond smile tugged at Diana's mouth. "My mother has mellowed considerably over the years, but back then she was what we call a militant feminist. She's still quite proud of the fact that she was one of the first to burn her bra in support of the Equal Rights Amendment.''

''She burned her bra?''

''Right on the steps of the U.S Capitol. As you might suppose, she encouraged my sisters and me to place comfort well ahead of fashion.''

Actually, Diana's avoidance of anything more constricting than an occasional sports bra was based more on her modest curves than her mother's militancy, but Stone didn't require that level of detail. She figured he'd discover soon enough that there were two classes of women in the modern world, those who enhanced their natural assets with underwire and permanent makeup, and those who couldn't be bothered.

Besides, he looked like he was having a difficult enough time with the basic concept of women's lib.

Poor baby, she thought wryly. He went down in the Father Knows Best era and had slept right through the entire sexual revolution. Wait until he found out about birth control pills and breast implants, not to mention the latest wonder drug for men.

Not that Charlie Stone would need it! Judging by the suspicious bulge in his borrowed pants, he was already supercharged.

To Diana's considerable surprise and annoyance, her own body responded in kind. Her pulse stuttered, then kicked up another notch. Under the thin long johns, her nipples tightened to stiff peaks.

This was absurd!

Ruthlessly, Diana suppressed the shivery sensation. She was here to do a job, one that demanded all her concentration. She'd be of no use to OMEGA or the major if she couldn't maintain a level of detachment. Reminded of her mission, she snagged her sweater from the side bar and nonchalantly tugged it over her head.

"I'll tell you what," she said as she raked her fingers through her hair. "I've got some leave time coming from my job. Maybe I should fly back to California with you."

"Why would you do that?"

"I agree with Dr. Goode. You're a scientific phenomenon. If you won't let us study you in a controlled environment, maybe you'll let me accompany you as a friend and sort of guide to the twenty-first century."

"A friend, huh?"

His gaze made another slow slide to her now-covered chest. When his eyes met hers again, the expression in their blue depths was unreadable.

"Is this an invitation, Dr. Remington?"

"I beg your pardon?"

"I don't know what folks call it where you come from," he said brusquely, "but in my neck of the country, the kind of show you just put on followed by an offer to teach a guy the ropes means only one thing.''

Oh, brother! Talk about mixed signals.

''Just what do you think I'm inviting you to do?''

''This, for starters.''

Stepping between her knees, he curled a knuckle under her chin. As he bent his head and brought his mouth down to hers, Diana weighed her choices. She could knock his arm aside and follow up with a brutally effective forearm to his throat, thus derailing her attempts to gain his trust. Or she could let Charlie Stone enjoy his first kiss in forty-five years.

Which is what she decided to do. The mission came first, after all.

Head tilted, lashes drifting down, Diana waited patiently for his lips to brush hers. She soon discovered Major Stone wasn't an aficionado of the fine art of lip grazing. He went right to mouth-on-mouth...with a skill that sent shock waves throughout her body. Steeling herself against the little explosions of pleasure he detonated under her skin, she waited out the kiss.

When he raised his head at last, it took everything she had to keep her expression bland.

''Are you finished?''

''Yeah.''

''Then I think we need to set matters straight. I wasn't putting on a show or coming on to you, nor do I want you to read a sexual connotation into my offer to accompany you back to California. For the record, I'm involved in a relationship.''

"What the heck does that mean?"

"It means I'm seeing a man. We're, uh, dating.''

Dating didn't come close to describing today's complex mating rituals, but it was the best she could do with her lips still tingling from Charlie Stone's kiss.

"And this guy isn't going to mind you going back to California with me?"

He might, if he knew about it. Although Diana and quiet, unassuming Allen hadn't yet discussed, much less agreed to, exclusivity, even he demonstrated a few male territorial characteristics at times.

She dodged the issue with a shrug. "Things are different these days.''

"They can't be that different.''

She didn't intend to argue the point. "The offer to act as your mentor is still on the table, Major Stone. Take it or leave it.''

Despite his long years of service, Charlie hadn't made a formal study of war. He'd been too busy fighting and flying to hit the military history books. But one of the fundamentals of warfare every soldier or sailor learns instinctively is to keep your opponent in your gun sights whenever possible.

His gut told him Diana wasn't the enemy. Hell,

he didn't even know if there *was* an enemy. But until he got the answers to a few more questions, he'd keep her well within his sights.

"I'll take it."

Chapter 5

The heat. Charlie remembered the heat. It rose in iridescent waves from the hard-baked Mojave sand. Everything in sight seemed to float above the shimmering, searing cloud.

It also sucked the air right from your lungs. Pausing on the steps of the sleek little air force jet that had transported him and Diana Remington to Edwards Air Force Base, California, he drew in a quick breath and squinted through his tinted aviator sunglasses.

He'd been issued the glasses and a hastily outfitted air force flight suit during the short stopover in Alaska. The lightweight green Nomex uniform and brown leather jacket felt strange to him after years of wearing heavier, clumsier gear. He'd insisted on keeping his own high altitude suit and helmet with him, though, as well as the Colt .45. He carried them now in a bag gripped tight in one fist.

As he surveyed the scene, relief shafted through him in swift, sharp spikes. There they were, the two mammoth hangars that had dominated Edwards's flight line since well before Charlie's time.

"Look familiar?"

Angling around, he flashed Diana a quick grin. "Like I never left."

That wasn't true, of course. He'd recognized the two massive structures instantly, but the size and variety of the aircraft parked on the apron dazzled him. Descending the final step to the tarmac, he did a slow one-eighty while the hot concrete burned through the soles of his boots.

Even if he'd *wanted* to, he couldn't deny any longer that he'd stepped into a whole new world. The space-aged craft all around him made a mockery of his stubborn refusal to admit the truth.

"Those are F-117s," Diana told him, descending the steps in his wake. "Stealth fighters."

Those black, swept-wing beauties were fighters? Charlie started to salivate.

Shading her eyes with one hand, his self-appointed tour guide to the twenty-first century pointed to a behemoth parked farther down the ramp.

"And that's a C-5 Galaxy. At least, I think that's what it's called."

Holy Moses! The thing had to be four stories high. Awed, Charlie did another sweep of the flight line while a blue AF sedan drove across the apron and pulled up at plane-side. A tall, trim colonel with blond hair bleached almost white by the fierce desert sun climbed out.

"Major Stone?"

Shifting his gear bag to his other hand, Charlie snapped to attention and whipped up his arm. The colonel returned the salute before reaching out to shake the major's hand.

"I'm Colonel Pollock, commander of the Test Pilot School. Welcome home."

The simple greeting triggered an avalanche of emotions for Charlie. Only now, with blessedly reassuring sights and sounds and smells all around him, could he finally put to rest the panic that had been clawing at his insides ever since he'd come awake. This he knew. This was *his* world.

Swallowing the boulder that seemed to have gotten stuck in his throat, he gripped the colonel's hand. "Thanks."

"We've got a team assembled to process your change in status."

Change in status? Charlie felt more at home by the second. Trust the military to blanket his astounding return from the dead in mundane, bureaucratic terms.

"The team has been read in," the colonel added. "They're all cleared at the highest security levels and can be fully trusted. Dr. Remington, I understand you're now senior scientist in charge of Project Iceman."

"Yes, I am."

The Iceman tag gave Charlie a jolt every time he heard it, but he had to admit it fit. So did the title blondie had assumed to explain her continued presence at his side. He still couldn't bring himself to completely trust her, still hesitated to share his own theories about what had brought his plane down, but he'd accepted one stark reality.

Right now, Diana Remington formed the only anchor in his otherwise altered universe.

"If you'll both come with me," Pollock said, "I'll drive you to your quarters. The processing team is waiting for you there."

The last "quarters" Charlie had occupied at Edwards consisted of one eight-by-ten room on the second floor of a wooden, World War II-era barracks. The small, airless cube had housed him and another pilot, leaving space for only iron bunk beds and metal lockers. The building's common latrine facilities were located down a rickety flight of stairs, and the only relief from the stifling heat came from the wind that whistled through the wooden shutters, bringing clouds of Mojave sand in with it.

The Distinguished Visitor suite Colonel Pollack ushered them to literally dropped Charlie's jaw. The living room boasted a circular leather sofa, marble-topped tables and an astonishing array of electronic equipment stacked in a wall unit. Sliding glass doors offered a spectacular view of the high desert. Two bedrooms opened off the living area, every bit as luxurious.

"Is this how air force officers live these days?" he asked incredulously.

"We wish," Pollock answered with a grin. "No, these are Distinguished Visitor quarters. We host everyone from princes to movie stars when the space shuttle lands, and they tend to expect something a little more comfortable than your average crew dog quarters."

The space shuttle. Charlie's glance riveted on a framed picture of the delta-winged vehicle. The material supplied by the recovery team had included pictures and information on the space program. He'd read that one of his old test pilot buddies, Deke Slayton, had gone into orbit, but the reality of space flight still hadn't sunk in until this moment.

Charlie's pulse leaped. Maybe, just maybe, he'd qualify for the program like Deke and get to fly one of those babies. Excited by the idea, he followed Pollock to the dining room, where a half-dozen military personnel had jumped to attention. Every blasted one of them, he noted wryly, had one of those toy computers propped on the table in front of them. Diana had carried hers all the way from the Arctic. No one, it seemed, could function these days without one.

Colonel Pollock made the introductions. Finance, personnel, operations, public affairs, the flight surgeon, the shrink, a medical tech, the chaplain.

"Would either of you like something to eat or drink before we get started?" the colonel asked the new arrivals. "The fridge is fully stocked, or we can call the Officers' Club and have them send over a couple of trays."

Charlie looked to Diana, who must have sensed how eager he was to reclaim his life. Shaking her head, she declined the offer.

"We ate box lunches on the plane. I'm okay for now."

"Fine, let's get to it. Major Stone, if you'll sit here, I think Captain Rivera gets first crack at you."

The slender, black-haired personnel officer waited until all parties were seated. Her dark eyes gentle, she slid a form across the table.

"This your copy of AF Form 2098, which officially changes your status from Missing and Presumed Dead to Present for Duty. I've already updated the master personnel data system."

"That's all it takes, huh? One piece of paper?"

"That's all." She gave him a moment to read the form before passing him several others. "This is a set of orders reassigning you to the Test Pilot School here at Edwards, and this is a request to convene a special promotion board. The board will assess whether you should have been promoted along with your peers at various stages in your career."

"There were a lot of folks who thought I was lucky to make major."

She responded with a smile. "Your record says otherwise, sir. I've calculated the number of promotion boards you missed. Given your date of rank of, uh…" She stumbled over the year, swallowed hard, spit it out. "Of 1951, you'll get a total of seventy-two shots to everything up to and including major general. Sign here, sir."

Charlie hadn't recovered from the shock of hearing that he'd be considered for promotion to general when the serious young finance officer hit him with an even greater whammy.

"I retrieved your pay records from the archives, sir. At the time your plane went down, you were drawing twenty-five hundred and six dollars a month, plus another thousand hazardous duty pay. You were missing for five hundred forty months, which means you're entitled to back pay in the amount of…"

His fingers flew over a small plastic pad with buttons. Charlie had just figured out that three-inch square was some kind of a miniaturized calculator when the lieutenant calmly announced the total.

"One million, eight hundred ninety-three thousand, two hundred and forty dollars."

"What!'

The finance officer tapped the plastic keyboard again. "Yes, that's right. One million, eight hundred ninety-three thousand, plus change."

Dazed, Charlie could only gape at the man.

"Colonel Pollock said you'd need an advance against the amount due, so I drew out two thousand in cash. The rest we'll deposit electronically when you establish a bank account. If you'll sign here, sir."

While the lieutenant counted out a stack of crisp new bills, Charlie caught Diana's glance.

"Looks like you'll be able to replace your Golden Hawk with a Porsche. A whole fleet of Porsches, for that matter."

The laughter dancing in her green eyes generated the craziest urge to reach over, bury his fists in her shoulder-length waves, drag her to him, and kiss the woman senseless. He hadn't touched her since that little session in the exercise room at the top of the world, but he wanted to. Lord, he wanted to!

With a wrench, Charlie turned his attention back to the business at hand. "All right, let's get to the important stuff. When do I climb into a cockpit?"

The flight surgeon exchanged a glance with the

shrink. Clearing his throat, the physician took the point.

"We can't put you back on flying status until we fully understand the physiological and psychological effects of your incarceration in the ice. That could take months, Major Stone. Or years."

"I've already lost all the months and years I intend to lose."

The doc looked to Colonel Pollock. Leaning forward, the senior aviator reinforced the flight surgeon's position.

"We also have to consider the fact that you've never flown today's high performance aircraft."

"I've flown the Dragon Lady. Cruising along at 65,000 feet for upwards of eight hours is about as high performance as you get."

"The U-2 has undergone at least five generations of modifications since the last time you handled the controls. You might recognize the airframe, but that's about all. Assuming the docs find you fit to fly, it would take you at least a year to re-qual on the new avionics and aeronautical systems. Then there's your age..."

"I'm only thirty-one."

"By your count," Pollock said evenly. "By ours, you're seventy-six. We'll have to get a special waiver from the Secretary of the Air Force, and she'll have to decide whether to put someone who's gone through what you have back in the cockpit of a multimillion-dollar aircraft.''

He hesitated, then laid the truth on the line.

''Senator John Glenn just rode into space again at the age of seventy-seven. NASA justified his flight by needing to study the effects of the aging process in a zero-gravity environment. But that was a second shot for a man with a whole pile of political clout behind him. If I were you, I wouldn't count on picking up your career where you left off.''

''Well, hell!''

Charlie sat unmoving while the world he'd just reentered crashed and burned around him for the second time.

A queer little ache started in Diana's chest as she watched a now-familiar mask come down over his face. After all he'd gone through, to be told he couldn't do what he'd done best—the only thing he'd ever *wanted* to do—had to be a crushing blow.

''Let the docs look you over,'' the colonel said quietly. ''Then I recommend you take some time to think about things. Use some of the leave you've accumulated over the past forty-five years, explore the present a little. You may decide there's something you'd rather do with the rest of your life than strap yourself into a cockpit.''

Pollock left unsaid that once the major's story broke, Charlie wouldn't have time to fly. Diana knew, if he didn't, that he'd be swamped with requests for appearances on talk shows, for interviews, for lectures. He'd no doubt pull down another couple of million for book rights to his incredible story, even more in movie options.

She chewed on the inside of her lip as Charlie absorbed the colonel's advice.

"You're right," he said at last. "I need to take a little time, look up some friends. Can your people track down a few individuals for me?"

If the air force couldn't, Diana certainly could. She made a mental note of the short list of names Charlie supplied the personnel officer. There were only four, three men and a woman.

"I'll get on this ASAP, Major."

Pollock rose. "That's about it for the paperwork side of things. The docs want at you now. Dr. Remington e-mailed them the recovery team reports.

"I transmitted them electronically," she translated, catching Charlie's blank look.

"We'll get out of their way and let them have at you," the colonel said. Once more he gripped Charlie's hand. "We're operating on your schedule here, Stone. You tell us when you're ready for Phase Two in Operation Iceman."

"Yes, sir."

The others filed out, leaving Diana and Charlie with the psychiatrist, flight surgeon and med tech. The docs had already poured over the biomedical data she'd transmitted but asked Charlie's consent to run more tests. This time, he agreed to cooperate.

An hour later, both docs agreed that Major Stone's physical condition and mental facility were astounding considering his ordeal in the ice. Folding his stethoscope into his bag, the flight surgeon surveyed the array of carefully labeled glass tubes and plastic specimen cups the med tech was storing in a carrying case.

"We'll take these samples right back to the lab, but I'll need to check you into the hospital to do a complete evaluation of your cardiovascular, pulmonary and musculoskeletel systems. We'll make that part of Phase Two," he added with a quick glance at Charlie. "After you've enjoyed some of that leave Colonel Pollack suggested."

Diana escorted them to the door and handed them each a business card. "I'd like you to e-mail me the lab results. I want to keep current on Major Stone's medical status."

"No problem, Dr. Remington." Fishing one of his own cards out of his uniform pocket, the flight surgeon passed it to her. "Just in case you need to reach me."

"Thanks."

When she went back into the living room, Charlie had opened the sliding glass doors and wandered out onto the flagstone patio. Hands planted on his hips, he stared at the slowly purpling dusk.

With the swift changeability of the high desert, the temperature had dropped with the sun. Little more than a pleasant warmth lingered as Diana stepped through open doors. While she suspected Charlie's thoughts absorbed him more than the view, she couldn't help drawing in a quick breath at the vista spread out before them.

The Mojave boasted a harsh beauty all its own. With L.A.'s choking blanket of smog some eighty miles distant, the sky glowed a deep, clear violet. A full moon hung suspended in the amethyst curtain, surrounded by a million stars that sparkled like Austrian crystals. Closer to earth, tall-stemmed Joshua trees lifted their short, spiky arms to the night. Yuccas and Spanish bayonet captured the gleam like silver swords in the shadows.

"I've never really seen the desert by moonlight," Diana murmured, breaking the silence. "It's magnificent."

He didn't respond for long moments. She thought the night had claimed him, but it was his past.

"There used to be a roadhouse not too far from here," he said finally. "The Happy Bottom Riding Club. Pancho Barnes, the aviatrix, opened it up during the war as a restaurant and bar catering to pilots. It closed before I left Edwards, but for years all the guys from the base used to congregate there. Jimmy

Doolittle, Chuck Yeager, Deke. We'd check out a jeep and drive across the desert, aiming for the lights.''

Diana didn't say a word. This was the first time he'd talked about himself, the first time he'd opened up.

''I closed the place one night. I was between missions and didn't have to fly the next day, so I plugged nickels into the jukebox and listened to Pancho's tales about her barnstorming days until she finally kicked me out. On my way back to the base, the jeep blew a gasket. I was too lazy to walk and knew the milk truck would make a dawn run, so I spent the night where I was. I remember the stars were just as bright as they are tonight, and the moon seemed to hang over me like a big, golden balloon.''

She held her breath while he turned, summoning a crooked grin.

''It's still hard for me to believe men have actually walked on the moon. And I missed it.''

''Oh, Charlie.'' Aching for all he'd lost, she laid a consoling hand on his arm. ''You've missed so much. I wish there was some way to give you back those years.''

Her sympathy seemed to embarrass the tough, ultramacho aviator. ''Yeah, well, right now I'll settle for a cold beer and a T-bone steak.''

''*That* we can manage. You grab a couple of

beers from the fridge and I'll take care of the steaks.''

"What's this? Are you actually going to turn on a real stove?"

"Not hardly. That's why the telephone was invented.''

She started to turn away, only to swing back when he caught her hand.

"Diana.''

"Yes?"

"I…"

The moment stretched. He looked so alone against the vast panorama of the stars, so lonely. His fingers tightened on hers. Calloused and warm, they sent little pinpricks of pleasure dancing up her arm.

"Thanks for listening," he said gruffly.

"You're welcome.''

She ached to comfort him. Ached to slide her arms around his waist and fit her body against his. Just the thought raised a flush on her skin. She only needed to take one step, a slight move forward, and she'd be in his arms.

Without warning, the need that had swept through her when he'd kissed her at the oceanographic station surged back, sudden and fierce. Surprised by its savage intensity, she took a quick, jerky step away.

"I don't know about you," she said with a breezy cheerfulness designed to cover her sudden, throat-closing desire, "but I'm ready for that beer.''

Chapter 6

Diana couldn't sleep.

Her internal clock was still shuffling between Washington, Arctic and California time. She tried to convince herself it was the two beers she'd downed with her steak that had left her so edgy and restless, but knew darned well the real cause of her sleeplessness.

He was sacked out in the next room.

Hoping a shower would relax her, she leaned against the tiled stall while hot, stinging pellets needled her from head to toe. When that exquisite torture didn't make her sleepy, she wrapped up in one of the inch-thick terry-cloth robes she found hanging behind the bathroom door, settled down at the desk in her bedroom, and flicked on her laptop. She might as well check her e-mail and get caught up with what was happening in her other life. She also needed to contact Allen and explain that she'd be out of town longer than she'd anticipated.

At the thought of her steady companion, something uncomfortably close to guilt fluttered along the edges of Diana's conscience. They hadn't made any promises to each other, she rationalized, certainly hadn't exchanged any pledges. Yet the fact that Allen had barely popped into her mind in the past few days bothered her.

That wasn't all that bothered her. She couldn't stop thinking about the needs Charlie triggered in her. They seemed to come on so fast, to build with such intensity. She'd have to axe this growing attraction to the man or...

Or what? Throw him down on the nearest horizontal surface and have her way with him?

Yes! the insidious little voice in her head whispered.

No! her conscience sternly rebuked.

That would be all Charlie needed. First his life turns inside out and upside down, then his only anchor to the twenty-first century decides to jump his bones.

Not that he'd mind, Diana thought wryly. She suspected Charlie would be more than willing to participate in his own seduction, but her sense of fair play wouldn't allow her to take advantage of his present isolation. Nor would it allow her to avoid the truth any longer. She cared for Allen Mc-Dermott...as a friend. She enjoyed his company...as a friend. But she had a bad case of the hots for the Iceman.

Sighing, she hit the e-mail icon and zapped out a quick message.

Hi, Allen—
This business is taking a bit longer than I expected. I'll call you when I get back in town. We need to talk.

Diana

A click of the built-in mouse sent the message out via the powerful wireless transmitter installed in all OMEGA's field computers. Feeling an odd sense of relief, Diana tapped a fingernail on the keys and listened with half an ear to the sounds outside. The busy base didn't shut down operations even at night. Jet engines whined in the distance, revving to an occasional blast of noise as the aircraft roared down the runway and lifted into the sky. Every once in a while, a car whooshed along the roads behind the Visiting Officers' Quarters.

The sound of the vehicles roused a ripple of curiosity. Idly, she hit the icon to connect to the World

Wide Web, then did a quick search for Studebaker Golden Hawk. She wanted to see what Charlie's pride and joy had looked like.

Two clicks later, there it was. Bright red, fin-tailed, dripping with chrome. The white walls had to be at least five inches wide. Smiling, Diana clicked on another Web site, then a third. Suddenly, her fingers froze on the trackball.

"Restored 1957 Studebaker Golden Hawk," she read breathlessly. "Engine completely recondi-tioned and in full compliance with California's emission control standards. Leather interior and spe-cial trim in primo condition. Offers now being ac-cepted. Andersen International Classic Cars, 661-326-4419."

Excitement snapped along her nerves. Her fingers flying, she clicked on a dozen more classic car pages and followed the links on those pages to twenty more. After an extensive hunt, she went back to the original Andersen page and pushed the stem of her functional black chronometer.

"Control, this is Artemis."

"I read you, Artemis."

She recognized Mackenzie Blair's voice instantly.

"Don't you ever go home, Comm?"

"I'll get a life one of these days," OMEGA's chief of communications drawled. "What's up?"

"I have a special request. There's a 1957 Golden Hawk advertised online by Anderson International

Classic Cars. They list a phone number of 661-326-4419.''

''That's a California area code. Bakersfield, I think.''

Diana heard the click of a keyboard.

''Yep, that's it. Bakersfield.''

Her excitement took another spike. Bakersfield was less than a hundred miles away!

Just a few hours ago, she'd ached to give Charlie back his lost years. She couldn't. No one could. But she could darn well give him back this piece of his past.

''Do me a favor and track down the site owner. If the car's still available, tell him we want to test-drive it pending a possible sale.''

''I take it this is for the Iceman.''

''You got it.''

''Okay, I'll get back to you within the hour.''

''If it's available, I want it delivered to the DV quarters at Edwards by eight o'clock tomorrow morning,'' Diana warned.

''I think we can manage that.''

''I also need you to contact the State of California DMV and have them issue a new driver's license in the name of Charles Stone. No doubt his old one has expired.''

''No doubt,'' Mackenzie said dryly.

''The DMV will want a home address. Use the Bachelor Officers' Quarters here on base as a temporary address. Major Stone can update the license when he decides where he wants to settle.''

"Consider it done. I'll have the necessary papers delivered with the car. Anything else, Artemis?"

"Yes. Would you check current status on these four people?"

From memory, she fed Mackenzie the names Charlie had mentioned to the personnel folks earlier.

"These won't take long. I'll furnish the information when I get back to you on the car."

"Thanks."

Signing off, Diana grinned and stretched like a cat. At times there were definite advantages to working for an agency like OMEGA.

Charlie woke to the sounds of jet engines revving. For a few seconds he drifted on a comfortable haze between sleep and consciousness. Thoughts bubbled up, percolating through his mind like air bubbles. He should roll out of the rack. Hit the showers. Check in with base ops. They would've sent a runner over if they'd laid on a short-notice mission, but it never hurt to...

His thoughts skittered to a stop like a jet with a heavy boot on the air brakes. Slowly, Charlie opened his eyes. Cradling his head in his hands, he stared up at the ceiling while reality crashed down with a vengeance.

There wouldn't be any runners from ops. No

short-notice missions. He wasn't in his bunk at Adana AB, Turkey, on call to fly highly classified intelligence-gathering missions over the Soviet Union. He was back at Edwards, sprawled across the biggest mattress he'd ever planted his butt on. And from the way the colonel had laid matters on the line yesterday, it might be a considerable stretch of time before he climbed into a cockpit again. If ever.

He was halfway through his rather considerable repertoire of four-letter words when Diana interrupted.

"Hey, Major," she called through the door. "It's after nine."

Her voice loosened the iron band that had clamped tight around Charlie's chest. Not all the way, but enough for him to answer when she wanted to know if he planned on getting out of bed today.

"I'm considering it."

"Well, get things in gear. I'm hungry, and there's no room service this morning. The club's closed. We'll have to go out for breakfast."

"Give me ten minutes to shower and shave."

As it turned out, what should have been simple, familiar acts took him almost half an hour. First he had to figure out how to adjust a showerhead that either drizzled limply or shot out a pulse sharp enough to put out his eye. Then he had to wrestle what was billed as a disposable razor from its wrappings. The damned plastic was sealed tighter than the rubberized neck rings on his helmet.

A lot tighter.

The grim reminder sent him back into the bedroom with a renewed sense of purpose. He might not have a flight scheduled today, but there was something just as critical he intended to get done.

Standing beside the bed with a towel wrapped around his hips, he ripped the wrappings from the clean skivvies and T-shirts he'd been supplied during the brief stopover in Alaska. The T-shirt was spun from soft, familiar cotton, but instead of the plain white jockey shorts of his day, these were a crazy purple color. Not only that, but the waistband sported the packager's name and logo in inch-high letters.

Why in the hell would advertisers stencil their name on underwear? What was the point when no one could see it? Shaking his head, Charlie pulled on his borrowed shirt, pants and socks before shoving his feet into his brown aviator boots. That done, he grabbed the gear bag containing his helmet and flight suit and headed for the door.

Diana was perched on a stool at the kitchenette's counter, coffee mug in hand. She wore her hip-hugging slacks and the red and green plaid shirt she'd had on when he'd first opened his eyes. Now, as then, the sight of her gleaming green eyes and finger-combed silvery blond waves sent his stomach into a quick spin.

"You've got time for one cup," she warned as he reached for the coffee maker to pour a shot. "Then we roll."

"Roll where?"

"I figure it's time to introduce you to the modern marvels of fast food. After that, we'd better hit the mall. The shopping center," she amplified at his puzzled look. "The temperature's supposed to reach ninety today. I don't know about you, but I'm ready to shed this heavy wool and get comfortable."

He downed a long swig of coffee. "After that, I want to visit some folks."

"Right." Reaching across the counter, she retrieved a printed sheet of paper. "Captain Rivera sent over this status report on the people you asked about."

Diana didn't mention that she'd augmented the captain's report with the more detailed information supplied by Mackenzie Blair this morning. OMEGA's communications chief had worked the short list herself and confirmed that two of the people on the list were dead. Of the others, one, the female, was currently off on a cruise with her husband of forty-four years and two of their seventeen grandchildren. Charlie's jaw locked as he skimmed the details provided by OMEGA.

"Was she a close friend?" Diana asked quietly.

He forced a shrug. "We knew each other during the war."

His one-time fiancée, she guessed. The nurse who'd mustered out and returned home to marry her high school sweetheart. Diana felt another twinge of pity for a man cast adrift from all his former friends as Charlie turned his attention to the fourth person on the list. An aviator turned engineer who'd retired from Lockheed's famous Skunk Works years ago, Harry Simmons now resided in Santa Monica.

"I recognize this address," Charlie said with a touch of relief mixed with determination. "Harry's folks used to live on Fourth Street. We'd visit them whenever we could get away from the base. His mom would always bake us a strawberry and rhubarb pie."

"Looks like they kept the house in the family. Your friend now lives there with his daughter."

Folding the list, he shoved it into his shirt pocket. "I need to get to Santa Monica."

"Not a problem. We can head for the coast after we hit the shopping mall. I've arranged for transportation. It's waiting outside."

While he downed the rest of his coffee, Diana snatched up the day organizer that held her civilian ID and credit cards. A bland smile was all she allowed herself as she and Charlie exited the DV quarters into dazzling sunshine.

The man at her side reached in his pocket for his

aviator sunglasses. The glasses in place, he took one step and stopped dead in his tracks. Stunned, he stared at the tomato-red convertible parked ten yards from the door.

Diana had to admit it was a beauty. Big and clunky by today's standards, but an undeniable work of art. Chrome bumpers gleamed. Five-inch white-walls glistened. In addition to its other accoutrements, the four-seater sported sleek silver rockets atop the front fenders and a pair of fuzzy dice hanging from the rearview mirror.

"You'd better drive," she said nonchalantly, digging a set of keys out of the side pocket of her day planner. "I haven't handled a standard in years."

He didn't say a word, not a word.

"It's not the same year as your baby," she admitted, dangling the keys. "I couldn't find a '56 for sale, but according to the literature, the '57 got a bigger, better V-8 engine."

Still Charlie didn't speak.

"The '57 was offered with four levels of accessories," she purred seductively. "This one has leather seats and special chrome interior trim. Check it out."

Like someone in a trance, he approached the convertible and ran his fingers along her fender.

What was it about men and cars? Diana thought with a smile. A less secure woman might feel just the tiniest dart of envy at the way he caressed the polished metal. Not to mention the adoration in his gaze as it roamed the interior.

"How did you find her?"

"On the computer. You can order everything from shoes to Studebakers online these days and have them delivered right to your door."

Airily, Diana glossed over the extreme measures OMEGA had employed to deliver this particular Studebaker to this particular doorstep by the time she'd specified.

"You've got her on approval," she warned. "You might not want to keep her when you hear how much she's going to cost you above original price tag of thirty-three hundred."

"More than a million-eight?"

"Not hardly!"

"Then I'll keep her."

"Just like that?"

"Just like that." He flashed her a grin. "I don't believe in idling my engines. When I see something I want, I go after it."

He looked so happy, like a kid at his own birthday party. With a matching joy feathering around the edges of her heart, Diana tossed him the keys.

"Okay, Stone, she's yours. Let me call and close the deal for you."

While she dug her cell phone out of her purse and called the private number OMEGA had supplied along with Charlie's updated driver's license, he slid behind the wheel. The Hawk's engine turned over with a well-mannered growl that quickly grew to a rumbling roar. Chrome exhaust pipes rattled. Dust and heat rose in swirls at the rear of the convertible.

Smiling, Diana finalized arrangements for payment and transfer of title. She was reaching for the door handle when Charlie jumped out.

"Hold on!"

With a courtesy she found oddly touching, he rounded the front end to open the passenger door for her. He swung it wide, but stepped in front of her before she could slide onto the seat.

"Looks like I owe you. Again."

"I'm not keeping a tab."

"I am. I like to pay my debts."

"Charlie, it's okay, really. All I did was surf the Web and make a few calls."

"If you say so." Sliding a hand through her hair, he tipped her head forward and delivered a quick, hard kiss. "Thanks, kid."

"You're, uh, welcome."

Her pulse skittering wildly, Diana climbed into the Hawk and immediately let out a yelp. Although it was just nine-thirty or so, the sun had already baked the white leather seat tar-paper hot.

The heat didn't appear to bother Charlie. Reclaiming his seat behind the wheel, he gunned the engine for another long, satisfying moment before asking for directions.

"Where's this place we're going for breakfast?"

"Just across base."

Toasted by sun and hot leather, Diana guided Charlie through his first experience with a fast-food drive-through. The attendant on headset waited patiently while he studied the menu and the cars backed up behind them.

"Try an Egg McMuffin and an OJ," Diana finally suggested. "That'll cover at least four of the five basic food groups."

After claiming their drinks and meal from the attendant at the second window, they parked under the shade of a feathery Russian olive tree. While Diana dug into the bag, Charlie observed the activity inside the glassed-in play place.

"I'm glad to see drive-in hamburger joints haven't gone out of style," he commented after a moment, "but in my day they didn't cater to kids. Just cool cats in black leather jackets and chicks wearing eight layers of petticoats and little chiffon scarves tied around their necks."

"Most of the cool cats and chicks hang out at the mall these days."

"The shopping center you told me about?"

"Right. The next stop on our itinerary. Eat up and we'll hit the road."

* * *

Getting *to* the mall proved as interesting an experience as shopping there.

The four-lane road leading out the front gate wasn't bad, but when they approached the ramp for the interstate, Charlie pulled over to the shoulder.

"What's that?"

Belatedly, Diana realized that he'd never seen a controlled access, high-speed highway before, much less three levels of concrete roadway wrapped in an intricate cloverleaf pattern.

"That's I-405," she answered. "It's a feeder to Interstate 5, which is part of the coast-to-coast interstate system."

"I knew President Eisenhower had started construction of a major highway system to replace Route 66," he said slowly, "but never imagined it would result in something like this."

Diana chose not to shatter his illusions by informing him that the nationwide network of highways Eisenhower had initiated was already severely overburdened and showing alarming signs of age. He'd find that out for himself soon enough.

"Do you want me to take the wheel?" she asked. "The traffic will turn nasty the closer we get to L.A."

"I can manage it."

"All right, hotshot." With a careless wave, she

committed them both to the concrete jungle. "Head straight south."

He quickly put to rest any worries about his ability to navigate the interstate. He and the Hawk might both be fifties vintage, but they came equipped with superb motoring and cornering skills. The reconditioned, souped-up Studebaker hugged the pavement, its heavy weight providing an unbelievably smooth ride compared to today's lighter, if more fuel-efficient vehicles. With the wind whipping her hair and the brown-green desert landscape rolling by, Diana didn't even mind the absence of air-conditioning. Much!

She was more than happy, though, when she spotted the signs for the Antelope Valley Mall. She desperately wanted out of her wool and into something cool and light.

So did Charlie. He made no effort to hide his amazement at the variety of stores congregated in the open-air, flower-filled plaza just outside town. Judiciously, Diana steered him past trendy boutiques geared to the younger set and into a well known, air-conditioned department store.

"My friend wants comfortable," she declared to the sales clerk in the men's department.

The clerk eyed Charlie's wide shoulders and lean hips. An appreciative gleam sprang into his eyes.

"We can do comfortable. We can certainly do

comfortable. With a build like your friend's,'' he gushed, ''we can do just about anything.''

From the corner of her eye, Diana caught the surprised and slightly wary expression that crossed Charlie's face.

Oh-oh. She reached for his arm, thinking to take him aside and bring him up to speed on the alternate lifestyles many men and women openly embraced today. Before she got the chance, the eager clerk whisked him toward the sports department.

She trailed in their wake, holding her breath, only to find that she'd once again underestimated Charlie. He set the fawning salesman straight using some form of silent communication that only males seemed to understand. With an audible sigh of regret, the clerk put a lid on his obvious interest.

''We just got in a new shipment of chinos and jam pants. If you'll come this way, sir.''

Twenty minutes later, they'd piled an assortment of slacks and knit polo shirts beside the register. Diana left the two men going through the shorts rack and dashed to the women's department. Three hastily crammed shopping bags later, she returned to find Charlie patiently waiting for her.

''Oh, my!''

Her footsteps slowed. Her heart did a crazy little somersault.

''Well?'' the clerk demanded with a proprietary

smirk. "Is he totally right for the California look, or what?"

"Totally," she breathed, lost in awe as she took in the neon orange flip-flops, khaki cargo shorts, and brightly flowered Hawaiian shirt.

"I hope I don't look as ridiculous as I feel," Charlie muttered, strolling forward to relieve her of her bags.

"You look…incredible."

And hip. And gorgeous. And astonishingly virile. After seeing the man naked, she wouldn't have imagined the mere sight of his muscular, hair-roughened calves below the hems of his baggy shorts would constitute such a turn-on!

"You look pretty good yourself," he returned. "I like the dress."

Diana was suddenly, absurdly pleased with her hurried purchase of a black and white polka-dot wrap-around. The slit in the dress's front opened almost to the thigh with each step. Teamed with strappy black sandals, the slinky little number made her feel cool, chic, and decidedly feminine.

Charlie gave her another slow once-over. "Can't say that your watch goes with the outfit, though. It's got more dials than an F-86."

"Functional beats dainty any day in my book," Diana said airily.

Not to mention the fact that Mackenzie Blair would have heart palpitations if Diana traded the clunky chronometer with all its embedded electronics.

Shifting her shopping bags to join those in his right hand, Charlie guided her through the aisles with his left. It was a hopelessly archaic gesture, but Diana had to admit she enjoyed the warmth of his palm at the small of her back.

Only after they'd tossed their bags in the convertible's back seat did she dig into her purse for her special purchase. Grinning, she knotted a small square of white chiffon around her neck.

"There. Do I fit the image of a real cool chick?"

"Almost." His mouth curved. "You forgot the crinkly petticoats."

"A girl has to draw the line somewhere. I'm not about to ride on this hot leather seat encased in six layers of itchy net."

His gaze slid down to the crossed legs exposed almost to the thigh by the slit in her sundress. When he raised his glance to hers again, the gleam in his blue eyes sent heat coursing through her veins.

"Actually, I like the current styles better. A lot better."

Diana's breath caught. It took her several moments to remember why she was sitting in an open convertible with the sun beating down on her head and shoppers sending curious glances their way.

A U-2 downed forty-five years ago under mysterious circumstances. A president who wanted the facts about that incident. A potential political imbroglio with Russia if and when those facts came out. With a mental shake of her head, Diana got back to the business at hand.

"You wanted to look up your friend in Santa Monica, remember? If you don't want to experience L.A. traffic at its worst, you'd better rattle these pipes, Major."

Chapter 7

They beat the afternoon rush hour, barely. Even at two-thirty, continuous streams of vehicles clogged the four-and five-lane freeways leading into the City of Angels.

Charlie's initial amazement at the number and variety of cars, all occupied by drivers with car phones glued to their ears, soon gave way to the grinding tension of stop-and-go traffic. A knot formed at the base of his neck and grew tighter with each mile they traveled.

Nothing on the outskirts of L.A. looked familiar to him. Nothing. Frowning, he searched in vain for recognizable landmarks amid the ocean of glass-fronted skyscrapers, the apartment complexes, the seemingly endless rows of stores Diana termed strip malls. Only the palm trees lining the streets and the occasional stucco cottage tucked among more recent structures recalled his era.

Inching west on I-10, they passed the maze of buildings that constituted Culver City on the right and the fringes of Hollywood on the left. Only after they'd exited the Santa Monica Freeway onto the Pacific Coast Highway did Charlie start to breathe again.

There it was, the shining, sun-capped Pacific. Waves rolled in, foaming onto the shore. The pounding, crashing surge was timeless. Ageless.

The Pacific, at least, hadn't changed. Nor had the famous Santa Monica Pier. Ignoring the traffic that backed up behind him, Charlie slowed the Hawk to a near crawl. Relief poured through him as he identified the structures on the wooden pier that jutted out into sea.

There was the same, neon-lit sign marking the end of Route 66, once the main highway stretching halfway across the country from Chicago to the promised land of California. And the carousel with its hand-painted horses, housed in a huge fantasy of a building constructed in Moorish style. He didn't remember the monstrous Ferris wheel, though, or the proliferation of restaurants and souvenir shops. Nor could he locate the vast, ornate La Monica Ballroom.

"There used to be a dance hall out on the pier," he told Diana as they cruised slowly by the jetty. "Whenever Harry and I hit Santa Monica, we'd stop by his folks' house first, then head for the pier to pick up townies and jitterbug half the night away."

Diana arched a brow. "I can guess what you fly-boys did the other half of the night."

"We rode the carousel," he drawled.

"Suuuure you did."

Charlie smothered a grin. He and Harry had racked up enough hits with the local girls to make the long drive in from Edwards well worth their effort. None of those curvaceous armfuls put a kink in his gut quite like the slender blonde sitting next to him, though.

He shifted uncomfortably on the leather bench seat as swift, erotic images from his former life leaped into his mind. He could see Diana sprawled beneath him on a blanket spread over the sand, her hair gilded by moonlight. Or curled next to him, her eyes luminous, as he parked the Hawk in a turnoff high above the Pacific. With a few smooth moves, he'd slither open the polka-dot dress and go to work on her underwear.

Which was when he remembered that Diana didn't wear a brassiere...

"Charlie, look out!"

With a silent curse, he jerked the wheel and re-turned the Hawk to its proper lane. Sweat dampened his palms. Beneath the baggy shorts, he was hard as a rock. Giving silent thanks for their excess of material, he aimed the Hawk along Ocean Boulevard.

On the left, the Pacific rolled into the shore. On their right, modern high rise hotels jostled for space alongside vintage resorts and B & Bs. Diana watched the side streets slide by for several moments.

"Don't you think we should call ahead and get directions from your friend? Or at least find out if he's home?"

"And tell him what? That his buddy who's been missing for almost fifty years wants to stop by for a visit? I'd rather just show up at his door and take my chances."

"It's your call," she said with a lift of her shoulders. "Can you find the house?"

"I think so." He squinted through his sunglasses at the palm-lined side streets. "It should be just off Washington Avenue."

"There's Washington," she pointed out a moment later.

Charlie swung the wheel and immediately experienced an unsettling sense of déjà vu. The neighborhood looked exactly the same as when Harry's folks lived there, yet so very different. The neat, thirites-era stucco cottages still marched down either side of the street. Red and orange hibiscus still spilled in wild profusion beside doors and driveways. But most of the houses boasted additions that doubled their size and almost half of them had weird little dishes perched atop their pitched roofs.

"Those are satellite dishes," Diana explained when he asked their purpose. "They can pull down anywhere from two to three hundred channels."

The idea that the average, ordinary Americans living right here on Fourth Street in Santa Monica, California, could receive signals from space disconcerted Charlie so much he drove right past six-ten. Recognizing his error, he hit the brakes. The white walls screeched in protest but brought the Hawk to a gliding halt.

With the engine idling, Charlie looped his wrists over the steering wheel and studied the house. The once dun-colored stucco was now flamingo pink and the palms in the front yard reached high into the blue sky, but an arched porch still shaded the entry and the faded turquoise shutters he remembered framed the windows.

"This is it," he said grimly, backing the Hawk up to the driveway. Now that he was here, the knot at the base of his skull torqued even tighter.

Harry Simmons was his only buddy still alive and well, the only peer from his time he trusted hands down. An aeronautical engineer by training and air force pilot by profession, Harry had worked with Lockheed to design the high-altitude flight suits required for the U-2 program. As an air force test pilot, Charlie had spent hours in the experimental suits even before he'd been detailed to the CIA to help transition the Dragon Lady into an operational aircraft. If anyone could help him make sense of those nightmarish last moments before he bailed out into the blackness, Harry could.

Slamming the convertible's door, he reached into the back seat for his gear bag. Diana was halfway out before he could get around to open her door. She gave the canvas bag a speculative glance as he reached down to help her out. Not even a flash of long, slender thigh lightened the tension that gripped Charlie as he ushered her up the front steps with a hand at her back.

The woman who answered the door was a short, stocky brunette with tired lines at the eyes and mouth and streaks of silver at her temples. Charlie assumed she was Harry's wife until he got a better look. With a jolt, he realized she must be his friend's daughter.

"Yes?" she asked through the screen door.

"We're looking for Harry Simmons."

Suspicion narrowed her eyes. "You're not from that publisher's sweepstakes, are you? I've already told them three times that dad didn't know what he was doing when he sent in those so-called winning tickets."

"I'm not..."

"If you think I'm going to pay for all those damned magazines, you can think again!"

Charlie blinked, taken aback by her vehemence. "I'm not a magazine salesman. I'm a test pilot. Or I was until recently," he amended gruffly.

Her gaze dropped from his flowered Hawaiian shirt to his orange shower clogs. "You don't look like a test pilot to me. What do you want with my dad?"

"I just want to talk to him about a special project we worked together on."

Her suspicion deepened. "Dad retired almost twenty years ago. If you worked with him, you couldn't have been more than five or six years old at the time."

"I've, uh, aged well."

Smoothly, Diana stepped into the breech. Digging her wallet out of her purse, she flipped open her ID. "I'm Dr. Diana Remington and this is Major Charles Stone. We're engaged in a special project for the United States Air Force and would like to ask your father a few questions about the work he did at Lockheed Aircraft."

The woman's shoulders sagged. "You can ask," she said wearily, pushing open the screen door. "Just don't expect many answers."

Leading them into the living room, she gestured to a rail-thin figure slumped in a wheelchair parked before a TV. Hearing their footsteps over the laughter of a game show, the chair's occupant lifted his head.

Charlie sucked in a ragged breath. He'd steeled himself to find Harry older, thinner, perhaps frailer. But not *this* frail, and not wearing this absent, vacuous smile. His chest tight, he walked over to the chair.

"Harry, it's me. Charlie Stone."

The empty smile stayed in place.

"We worked together on that…that high altitude aircraft at Lockheed, remember?"

Even now, the name of the super-secret plane got stuck in his throat. Hunkering down beside the wheelchair, he gripped the gear bag tightly in his fist.

"You helped design a special flight suit, and I tested it during air trials."

Reaching out a shaking hand, Harry patted him on the cheek. "Thatzniz."

"What?"

Charlie received another fumbling pat.

"Thazniz."

Frowning, he swiveled on his heels. Harry's daughter interpreted in a voice that combined love, anguish and painful resignation. "He said, 'That's nice.' That's all he *can* say anymore."

Diana moved to her side, her face awash with pity. "Is it Alzheimer's?"

When the older woman nodded helplessly, Charlie pushed to his feet and crossed to the room. "Who or what is this Al Himers?"

"It's a progressive disease of the neurological system," Diana explained softly. "It primarily affects the elderly, although there are numerous cases involving people in their middle years. We only recognized the disease a decade or so ago and are still searching for a cure."

"You mean there's no treatment?"

"No. The victims usually lose their memory first, then their motor skills. Eventually they..."

"They die," Harry's daughter whispered, her eyes shimmering. "Without knowing who or where they are, or remembering even their own names. The doctors don't give dad more than a few more months."

Swallowing the rock-hard lump in his throat, Charlie returned to his friend and gave Harry's hand a gentle squeeze.

"Sorry you're under the weather, buddy. I'll come back when you're feeling better. Maybe... Maybe we'll talk about old times."

"Thazniz."

Diana kept silent as Charlie backed the Hawk down the drive. Slowly, he retraced their route down Washington Avenue toward the ocean. He stared straight ahead, his hands fisted tight on the steering wheel, the knuckles showing white.

The breeze off the Pacific whooshed through the tall palms lining the street. The June sun warmed the air, but Diana wrapped her arms around her waist and fought off a shiver. She didn't know who she felt worst for. Harry Simmons had lost his memory. His daughter had lost her father. Charlie had lost everyone.

Diana wanted desperately to comfort him, almost as much as she wanted to ask him why he'd lugged the canvas gear bag down to L.A. His high altitude flight suit had some connection to the loss of his plane. That was becoming painfully obvious. But what?

She'd examined the gear at the oceanographic station, as had Dr. Goode and the rest of the team. Aside from the rubber seals that had disintegrated when exposed to air, the flight suit had survived the incarceration in the ice remarkably well. So why had Charlie wanted to talk to the engineer who helped design the equipment? And when would he trust Diana enough to share his thoughts?

When the Hawk nosed onto Ocean Avenue once more, she stared blindly at the waves curling in on the shore. She'd better report to Lightning ASAP, ask him to put Comm to work researching all material related to the U-2 pilots' flight gear. If anyone voiced questions or concerns about the equipment at the time of Charlie's disappearance, Mackenzie Blair would dig them up.

Lost in her thoughts, she didn't notice Charlie had slowed the Hawk until he pulled into a parking turnout alongside the beach.

"I need to walk," he said gruffly.

"Do you want company?"

He shrugged. "If you can manage the sand in those shoes."

"Not a problem." Toeing off the strappy sandals, she reached for the door handle.

"Wait a moment!" he snapped.

Slamming his own door shut, he came around the front of the car. As much as she appreciated the courtesy, Diana debated whether to clue him in to the fact that today's women were perfectly capable of exiting a vehicle on their own. Later, she decided. He'd already been dealt one severe setback today. Tucking her sandals into her purse, she wiggled her toes in the hard-packed sand while he locked their purchases and his gear bag in the trunk.

They walked side by side. Shoulders hunched, hands thrust deep in his shorts pockets, Charlie let Diana set both the direction and the pace. The frisky breeze swirled her polka-dot sundress. She could practically feel the salt spray frizzing her hair.

With the damp sand tickling her soles, she charted a path through joggers, kite flyers, yoga enthusiasts, dog walkers and surfers, all out to enjoy the sun and the shore. Charlie speared a hard glance at the circle of purple-robed meditators, but it was the dog walkers who finally broke his brooding silence.

"Why are they all carrying those jugs?"

She glanced at the gallon milk jug carried by a Doberman owner. The bottom of the plastic container had been cut to form a convenient scoop.

"That's a pooper-scooper. There's probably a city ordnance that requires owners to clean up after their pets."

"You're kidding, right?"

"No, why would I? I don't know about you, but I'm not particularly keen about stepping in a steaming pile of doggie-do while strolling on a public beach."

"So you step around it."

"Folks are more environmentally conscious these days."

"What's more environmental than manure?" Thoroughly disgusted, he shook his head. "Next thing you know, you'll have to keep cats on leashes and put diapers on carriage horses."

"As a matter of fact…"

He shot her an incredulous look, opened his mouth, clamped it shut. Shaking his head again, he pushed on. Diana walked with him, knowing his edgy temper didn't have anything to do with dog poop or the unforgivable sin of opening her own car door.

She was feeling the pull of sucking sand in the

muscles of her calves and thighs when he finally steered her toward a weathered cedar bench on the boardwalk. Crossing his arms and ankles, Charlie contemplated the sea. Diana dusted off the soles of her feet and stretched out comfortably at his side. He'd talk if and when he was ready. Until then, she'd enjoy the view.

The sun blazed lower now, transforming the Pacific into a lake of bright, liquid gold. The receding tide left bits of shell and seaweed glistening on the wet sand. She tipped her head, trying to place the tune pumped out by the carousel's organ. Handel, she thought, from his *Water Music* suite.

An ominous rumble originating in the vicinity of Charlie's midsection pulled her from the joyous cascade of notes and him from his private thoughts. Stirring, he agreed with her solemn pronouncement that it had been a long time since their fast-food breakfast.

"There used to be a great seafood restaurant on the pier. Capn' Dave's Shrimp Boat, or something like that." Scraping a hand along his jaw, Charlie eyed the wooden structure jutting out into the sea. "It's probably long gone."

"If it is," Diana said briskly, "I'm sure another restaurant has sprung up in its place. Come on, let's find out."

Later, much later, Diana would wonder how she could so severely underestimate the impact of a bucket of u-peel-'em shrimp crunched down while watching the sun blaze into the Pacific. Or the magic of a ride on a hand-painted horse, followed by an hour of dancing under the stars.

If the image of Charlie's broad shoulders framed in a blaze of red and gold as he feasted on the shrimp didn't warn her of what was to come, the carousel ride certainly should have. By mutual agreement, they put aside their private concerns when they climbed onto their chosen steeds. Diana sat demurely sidesaddle while Charlie slipped his feet into the stirrups and folded his knees up almost to his chin. Grinning at his contortions, she grabbed the reins as the merry-go-round started slowly and gathered speed with each turn. Kids giggled and kicked their mounts' flanks and waved to parents. The music pouring through the loudspeakers was almost deafening at close range, yet the pumping melody started an answering rhythm in her veins.

Diana's blood was still singing when the ride ended. Legs spread wide against the moving floorboards, Charlie spanned her waist to lift her down. She braced her hands on his forearms and slid out of the saddle.

His muscles bunched under her fingertips. Hers contracted in instant, breath-shattering response. The music wheezed and died, but Diana's heart was hammering so loudly she didn't notice. For a moment she hung suspended between the unyielding wooden horse behind her and the equally unyielding body in front of her.

"Charlie..."

He squeezed her waist. "Listen!"

"Okay, I'm listening."

She wasn't sure what she expected at that moment, but it wasn't the crease that appeared in his forehead as he cocked his head and strained to hear the distant notes of a trombone.

"'So Tired,'" he muttered.

"Well, put me down."

Grinning, he planted her feet firmly on the wooden deck. "That's Russ Morgan's theme song. 'So Tired.'"

"Oh."

She'd never heard of Russ Morgan, but the slow, mellow slide of the trombone started a fresh set of goose bumps up and down her arms. They piled right on top of the ones Charlie's touch had already raised.

Grabbing her hand, he led the way through the crowd. "We have to find out where that music's coming from."

It came, they discovered a few moments later, from the open-air pavilion located at the far end of the pier. The banner strung above the pavilion's entrance proclaimed that the city was celebrating the history of the old La Monica Ballroom with a series of summer concerts, big band-style. This week's concert showcased the golden tones of Russ Morgan and the Morganaires.

"Thank God good music like this didn't go out of style," Charlie said in heartfelt relief. "Those hard rock CDs you played for me may be all right for teenagers, but this is the real thing."

Wisely, Diana refrained from informing him that the big band sound had faded from popularity decades ago and was just beginning to make a comeback.

As was swing dancing. Couples of all ages glided around the roped-off dance area. Most were gray-haired, but a respectable number of pairs from Generation X swayed to the clear, liquid notes. The dancers wore everything from cutoffs to polyester pants suits. However they were garbed, they all appeared to be enjoying themselves.

Her hand still tucked in Charlie's, Diana observed their moves with genuine admiration. Her fiercely liberal mother had refused to push her daughters into traditional activities like ballet or pom-dancing, insisting instead they follow their own inclinations to uncover their hidden talents. Diana's inclinations had led her to science fairs and biology labs, not dance classes, but she could still appreciate artistry in movement when she saw it.

Charlie, it turned out, intended to do more than just appreciate. After watching the dancers with a critical eye, he tugged her on her hand. "Come on, Doc. Let's show 'em how it's done."

She hung back, alarm rapidly replacing her admiration. "You can't dance in those flip-flops."

"Sure I can. It won't be a pretty sight, but we're not trying for Fred and Ginger here."

"Wait, Charlie! I don't know how to dance. Not like that, anyway."

"You don't have to know. I lead, you follow. And I'll have you know, I'm a good leader."

With that bit of totally oblivious chauvinism, he swung her onto the floor and into his arms.

Grudgingly, she was forced to admit he was a *very* good leader. His arm snug around her waist, he left no doubt about who was in charge of this operation. After the first stumbling steps, Diana fit her body against his and surrendered to his superior skill. Soon they were dipping and swaying with the rest of the crowd.

She had just congratulated herself on being a quick study when the slow, dreamy song ended. The orchestra segued right into something considerably more lively, and Diana's false sense of confidence took a direct hit.

"'The Johnson Rag'!" Charlie's blue eyes gleamed. "This came out when I was still in the Aviation Cadets. Hang on to your hairpins, sweetheart."

"I don't think I'm ready for this!"

"Sure you are. Just go wherever I throw you."

"Throw me?"

She aimed a quick glance at the other couples. Several women were already airborne. Swung high by their partners, they kicked their heels in midair and came down with an energetic bounce. One even slid feet-first right through her partner's legs.

"I *know* I'm not ready for this," Diana exclaimed, dragging at the hold on her hand.

"What's the matter?" Charlie cocked a brow. "Don't you trust me to catch you?"

The challenge hovered between them. Instant. Direct.

Trust. She wanted trust. She had to give it to get it.

"All right." She made no effort to hide her profound reluctance. "But I'm going to hold you directly responsible for any sprained ligaments or broken bones."

"We won't try anything *too* jive."

Armed with that less than reassuring promise, she joined the fray. After a few false starts, she got the hang of it, more or less. She even managed not to trip over her own feet when Charlie raised his arm, twirled her three times, and swung her back against his chest. She landed with a little ummph, breathless and laughing and totally energized.

So energized, in fact, that it was Charlie and not Diana who stumbled halfway through the next number. He recovered smoothly, but guided her off the floor at the end of the piece.

"Are you okay?" Diana asked, noting the white lines that bracketed his mouth.

The lines disappeared in a rueful smile. "You were right. These shower clogs aren't made for cutting a rug. Either that, or forty plus years on ice took more out of me than I realized. I'll have to find a workout machine like the one you showed me at the oceanographic station and get back in shape."

"I saw about all there is to see of your shape, fella, and it looked pretty darn good to me."

Unfortunately, she forgot that Charlie's frame of reference for banter between the sexes differed considerably from hers. She'd also put more of her own feelings into the quip than she'd intended. He looked startled, then thoughtful as his gaze traveled from her flushed face to the polka dots clinging to her upper breasts.

"It's a long drive back to the base." His hand moved in a lazy, seductive circle at the small of her back. "What do you say to spending the night in Santa Monica?"

Chapter 8

The half-mile drive from the pier to the hotels fronting Ocean Boulevard was one of the longest of Diana's life. When Charlie pulled into a plush resort with a sign proudly announcing the charm of vintage, beach-side bungalows updated with every modern luxury, she didn't say a word. She didn't have to.

She knew what would happen when they locked the door to one of those bougainvillea-draped cottages, knew she was about to break every rule in the undercover operative's book. Yet her pulse pounded with such urgency that she could scarcely breathe, much less remember the damned rules.

The hard truth was that she ached for Charlie

every way a woman could for a man. Almost from the day, from the very hour she'd walked into the makeshift lab and seen him lying on the metal table, he'd tied her in knots.

Physically, he turned her on, big time! Despite her stern lectures to herself, the biologist had somehow given way to the woman. For the first time in her life, Diana was discovering the powerful pull of the male physique. Or at least the male physique as embodied in one Major Charles Stone. For reasons that defied scientific analysis, he called to everything that was female in her. Her first glimpse of his naked body had started her hormones working overtime and they'd yet to take a break. Just thinking about what would happen when they checked into one of the beachside bungalows sent tight, clenching spasms through her lower belly.

But what she felt for Charlie went deeper than mere physical attraction. Far deeper. Emotionally, he plunged her from the dizzying heights of sexual excitement and scientific discovery to piercing hurt over his lost years. She'd never felt this aching sense of loss before, never shared another's confusion and struggle to find himself so intensely. With a slight kink in logic, Diana longed for Charlie to trust her with his secrets, even as she dismissed as totally irrelevant the fact that she harbored more than a few of her own.

Speaking of which...

A sideways glance confirmed that Charlie had disappeared inside the resort's elegant front entrance. Quickly, she keyed the radio encased in her watch.

"Control, this is Artemis."

"Go ahead, Artemis."

She might have known Mackenzie would still be at headquarters. Swiftly, Diana reported the sudden change in plans.

"We're not going back to Edwards tonight. We're staying in Santa Monica."

"Roger, Artemis. I put your present location at…"

With a few clicks of a mouse, Mackenzie verified the information being transmitted by the tiny global positioning signaling device in the black chronometer.

"The Pacific Shores Resort, on Ocean Boulevard, Santa Monica."

"Correct."

"How long a stay do you anticipate?"

"I don't know. A day. Maybe two. Major Stone needs some time to think things through."

So did Diana, for that matter, but the moment Charlie had started tracing those small circles in the small of her back, thinking had dropped to second or third place on her list of priorities.

"I can have someone out there in less than an hour to run a sweep of your rooms."

"I don't think that's necessary, Comm. For one thing, this stop was unplanned. For another, we're only getting one room. I'll, uh, maintain positive surveillance of the subject while we're here."

A short, startled silence ensued, but Mackenzie, bless her, refrained from editorial comment. That would come later, Diana suspected. From Lightning. She'd worked with Nick often enough in the past to know the flintlike edge he buried under all that sophisticated charm.

"Let us know if you need anything, Artemis."

"Roger. Now for Pete's sake, go home, Comm."

"I will, I will."

The woman needed to cultivate some outside interests, Diana thought. Preferably of the male persuasion. Maybe when she got back to Washington, she'd introduce Mackenzie to one of Allen's friends and...

Her thoughts skittered to an abrupt stop. Allen was over. If she'd harbored any lingering doubts about terminating her casual relationship, they'd gone up in smoke when she decided to stay in Santa Monica with Charlie. All that remained was a fierce impatience that mounted exponentially until the Iceman slid back behind the wheel.

With a glance in her direction that ignited the embers already smoldering in her blood, he keyed the ignition. The very air around her seemed to heat as he drove to the very last unit on the resort grounds. The cottage sat by itself on a small cliff some fifty or so feet above the beach. Rocky projections covered with ice plant and a few stubborn sea oats cut the cottage off from the others and gave it a sense of splendid isolation.

While Charlie retrieved his gear bag and their purchases from the trunk, Diana stood in the evening mist and gazed at the waves foaming the shore. A wooden staircase zigzagged down the cliff, inviting long walks and lazy hours on the narrow beach. Tomorrow, she thought. Maybe tomorrow they'd leave a trail of footprints in the sand or dig for shells. Tonight...

Tonight belonged to Charlie.

The man filled her mind, her thoughts, her senses. As she preceded him up the crushed shell walk to the cottage's door, every nerve snapped with expectation. Like electrical sparks shooting along an exposed wire, excitement danced all through her body.

The interior of the cottage only added to her simmering anticipation. The snug, cheerful rooms were designed for pleasure, and furnished for feet-up comfort. Pink-and-green plaid covered the love seat in the sitting room, with a matching flowered chintz for the overstuffed chair. The walls of the kitchenette sported framed prints of gaily painted carousel horses looking much like the ones she and Charlie had ridden not long ago. Sliding glass doors led from the sitting room onto a weathered cypress deck perched high above the ocean. From what Diana could see of the oversized bedroom beyond, it boasted a king-sized bed covered in the same pastel colors and a bank of windows that would offer a spectacular view of the Pacific in the morning.

It was the kind of place to cuddle up in, to watch the sun set over the ocean, and make love in all night long. As eager as Diana was to do just that, she didn't ignore the basics of her business. A swift visual security check showed sturdy latches on the sitting room windows. A dead bolt provided backup on the front door. The small kitchenette allowed no access from outside. She didn't like the sliding glass doors leading to the deck. They were too hard to defend against. Anyone determined to get into the place could simply break the glass. Or kick in the front door, for that matter. Both had happened at various times in Diana's past. She didn't expect either to occur here but worked out the appropriate responses and emergency escape routes in her mind just in case.

The rustling of paper brought her head around. All thoughts of escape fled as Charlie deposited the shopping bags in a careless pile atop his canvas bag. Straightening, he faced her across a few yards of plush gray carpet.

"I'm not sure how this is done these day. Do you make the first move, or do I?"

He was learning. If the blue flames in his eyes

were any indication, he wanted to jump her bones as much as she did his, but he was learning. Sliding her tongue along suddenly dry lips, Diana suggested a compromise.

"I'll tell you what. Let's meet halfway and see what happens."

Until that moment, Charlie had intended to take things slow and sweet. He'd imagined this moment too often in the past few days, had gone rock hard at the mere thought of burying his hands in that Jean Harlow hair and claiming her mouth with his to rush matters. The seductive sweep of Diana's tongue along her lower lip exploded his carefully laid plans in midair.

"To hell with halfway," he growled, crossing the few yards between them in two swift strides. "I've always gone the distance."

She welcomed him with a grin and open arms. Their bodies collided, thigh to thigh, hip to hip. Greedily, his mouth found hers. Just as greedily, she stretched up on tiptoe and locked her arms behind his neck. She made no attempt to disguise her hunger, played no coy games.

Her honesty literally took his breath away, but it was the erotic press of her hips against his that had his hands fumbling with the ties of her dress. The slinky fabric parted a moment later, and Charlie lost what little air he'd managed to suck into his lungs.

All she wore under the polka dots was a tiny triangle of black lace.

Sweat beaded his brow. His throat went bone dry. With a fervent prayer of thanks, he consigned the baggy cotton women's underpants of his day to whatever grave they'd been buried in. Before he could get the dress off her shoulders and all the way down her arms, she went to work on his shirt. The feel of her tongue hot and eager on his chest snapped the last of Charlie's already shaky control.

The dress caught on her elbows. His shirt dangled from one of his. In a snarl of arms and legs, they dropped to the plush carpet. He hit first to absorb the impact, then rolled Diana under him. With another heartfelt prayer of thanks for the absence of a brassiere, he claimed one of her firm, high breasts with his mouth. His tongue and teeth soon teased the nipple into a hard, tight peak.

"Ohhh! Oh, Charlie!"

Gasping, she arched under him. The movement gave him just the right leverage to drag down the scrap of lace. Wiggling frantically, she raised her hips the extra inch he needed to get rid of the panties—if you could call them that!—completely.

"Your turn," she said hoarsely, her fingers fumbling with the snap to his khaki shorts. He kicked them away a few seconds later, along with the orange shower shoes and ridiculous purple jockey shorts.

Whatever doubts had lingered in the back of Charlie's mind about present-day mating rituals disappeared the moment he covered her naked body with his. The instincts that gripped them both at that moment were as old as time, as unchanging as the sea.

His mouth ground down on hers. Her tongue warred with his. He cushioned his weight on his forearms to keep from crushing her, but she locked her heels around his calves, urging him, inflaming him.

Every muscle and tendon strained when he eased to one side and slid a hand between her thighs. Eagerly, she opened for him. One probe of his fingers told him she was ready, so ready that Charlie nearly fired his missile right then and there. Conquering the urge with an act of sheer willpower, he slid another finger into her slick depths and primed her even more. He was panting almost as hard and fast as Diana when her hand closed over his rigid flesh.

"Ho-ly cow!"

Her hand stilled. For a moment, laughter replaced the daze in her green eyes.

"Holy cow? Is that good or bad?"

"That's good, babe. Definitely good!"

With another gurgle of laughter, she tightened her fingers and slid them upward to cowl the tip of his shaft. Pleasure sliced through him, so fierce and sharp he had to jackknife away to keep from embarrassing himself. With a wicked smile, she held on.

Charlie withstood her torment as long as he could before he grabbed her wrist and pinned it to the carpet above her head. Positioning himself between her thighs, he thrust home.

With an eager lift of her hips, Diana welcomed him. She'd been right, she thought on a gasp. Major Charlie Stone definitely didn't need the latest wonder drug for men. He stretched her, filled her, completed her.

The idea startled her, but this was hardly the time or the place to stop and examine it. Shoving aside any and all attempts at rational thought, she gave herself up to the incredible sensations Charlie was generating with his hands and his mouth and his body. Soon—too soon!—she felt her climax begin to build low in her belly. Like the ocean outside, wave after wave of delight surged, ebbed, surged again.

A groan ripped from far back in Diana's throat. Arching, she rode the crest of her wild, swirling pleasure. The waves were just about to crash down when she felt Charlie stiffen. Moaning, she clenched her belly muscles, urging him to finish.

Abruptly, he flexed his hips and withdrew.

Diana's eyes flew open. Through a swirling haze, she took in the grim set to his jaw.

"Charlie?"

"Don't move."

Remembering how he'd staggered on the dance floor earlier, she felt a frisson of alarm and tried to wiggle up. "What's the matter?"

"Don't...move!" Sweat sheened his forehead. His chest heaved. The muscles on his upper arms quivered. "I promise...I won't leave you like this. And I won't...get you pregnant. I...just need...a minute."

Diana blinked. Good grief! He was trying to protect her. Evidently he had every intention of bringing her to a climax, but not himself.

Something soft and tender blossomed in her chest at that moment. Not love. It couldn't be love, she assured herself. More of an odd sort of affection.

She just wasn't used to being protected. Or having doors opened for her, for that matter. If her mother's radical feminism hadn't weeded out any and all inclination toward helplessness, Diana's OMEGA training would certainly have done the trick. Still, she felt the strangest, silliest melting when she cupped his cheeks in her hands and explained that coitus interruptus didn't work. Nor did the rhythm method, which is why they invented the birth control pill.

"There's a pill now?"

"Actually, there's something better than a pill. A shot that lasts for several months."

"Several months, huh?"

He thought about that for a few moments, then slid an arm under her hips. With one swift tug, positioned her under him once more.

"Maybe we should plan on staying longer than one night."

"Maybe," Diana gasped as he entered her, "we should."

She drifted out of sleep the next morning, lured into reluctant wakefulness by the nippy air and restless murmur of the sea outside the window.

It was June, for heaven's sake, yet the ocean breeze carried a distinct bite. Thankfully, Charlie's determination to make the most of the latest advances in birth control had—eventually!—landed them in bed.

A nice, warm bed, with a firm mattress and lightweight covers. Tugging on the blankets, Diana curled into a tight ball. In the process, she felt her knee collide with warm flesh. Poking her head out from under the covers, she pried open one lid. A naked chest rose and fell mere inches from her nose.

"Hi."

The rumbled greeting came from just above her head and chased away the last of Diana's morning fog. Uncurling, she rolled onto her back and tucked the blanket under her arms. A quick shove pushed her tangled hair out of her eyes.

"Hi, yourself."

Charlie lay beside her in a comfortable sprawl, his head propped on one hand. Stubble shadowed his cheeks. His brown hair stood in spikes. In the hazy light filtering through the curtained windows, he looked rugged, sleep-deprived, and all male.

And just a little remote.

A smile creased his cheeks, but it didn't quite reach his eyes. Diana hadn't expected a wake-up kiss, didn't *want* one until she'd made a dash to the bathroom, but neither had she thought that he would be the one to ease back a step or two after the wild intimacy of the night before.

A little piqued, she cocked her head. "What are you thinking about?"

"The fellow you said you're dating, for starters."

Surprised, she gave him a considering look. Was this a guy thing? Did Charlie feel he'd violated some kind of masculine code of honor by sleeping with a woman who might be involved with another man? She had no clue how the fifties male thought about such matters, but evidently was about to find out.

"Why are you thinking about him?" she asked curiously. "Are you feeling guilty?"

His smile knifed into a swift, predatory grin. "The *last* thing I'm feeling right now is guilty. If this friend of yours isn't man enough to hang on to his woman, he didn't deserve her in the first place."

His woman? Diana's lips curled in a moue of

distaste. She didn't find Charlie's chauvinistic tendencies quite as endearing this morning. Allowing him to open the door for her was one thing. Hearing him catalogue her as a trophy was something else again.

"What about you?" he asked, his eyes shadowed behind the screen of his lashes. "Are you feeling guilty?"

"No," she informed him coolly. "I've already e-mailed Allen and told him we have to talk when I get home."

"You 'have to talk?' What is that, some kind of twenty-first century code for take a hike, pal?"

"More or less."

"I'll remember that."

This wasn't at all the conversation she'd expected to be having after collecting carpet and/or whisker burns on both sets of cheeks. Humping her arms over the covers, she tipped Charlie a cool glance.

"You said you were thinking about Allen *for starters.* Who or what else is on your mind?"

His pulled in a deep breath, let it whistle out through his teeth. The rise and fall of the naked chest just inches from her nose distracted Diana momentarily.

"Do you have access to a lab?"

Her gaze snapped back to his face. "I have access to several."

A magnificent understatement, to say the least.

Her position at the prestigious Harrell Institute provided entrée to a host of private and educational research facilities. More to the point, her work for OMEGA allowed her to draw on the resources of highly classified government technical centers.

Charlie's blue eyes drilled into hers. "Can you request a special analysis? Have it done with no questions asked, and no reports provided to anyone but you?"

With a sudden pulse of excitement, she sensed he was about to share the secret he'd been guarding so closely.

"That can be arranged."

"Wait here. I'll get my gear bag. I want to show you something."

Only after he'd rolled out bed, dragged on his shorts, and headed for the sitting room did it dawn on Diana that last night had constituted some kind of a test. One she'd obviously passed.

The air left her lungs on a hiss. She slumped back against the chintz-covered headboard, her ego deflating at the same velocity as her lungs.

Smart, Remington. Real smart. Compromise your mission. Forget why you were sent to the Arctic. Jump into bed with the man you're supposed to protect, then feel hurt and used and *stupid* for doing it.

What the heck was the matter with her? She'd set out to win Charlie's confidence. That was the plan right from the start. So why should she feel like she'd just swallowed a giant fur ball?

Dammit all, anyway!

Shoving aside the covers, Diana swung out of bed and marched into the bathroom.

Chapter 9

He could trust Diana.

Right now, she was the *only* one he really trusted in the twenty-first century.

The thought hammered in Charlie's head as he retrieved his canvas gear from the sitting room. Tangled covers, an empty bed, and the drum of the shower against the bath tiles greeted him when he returned to the bedroom.

Duty clashed instantly, fiercely, with desire. He had to resolve the doubts he'd carried around with him since waking up in the Arctic. Needed answers to the questions that swirled constantly in his head. But a mental image of water sluicing down Diana's naked body short-circuited every instinct but the urge to slide into her warm, slick depths again. And again. And again.

Tossing his gear bag onto the bed, he started across the room. He was halfway to the bath when the water cut off. Reluctantly, he wrestled his rampaging lust into submission. He had no idea what morning rituals women performed these days, but he suspected Diana might prefer privacy while she powdered or puffed or whatever. What's more, he acknowledged, scraping a hand along his jaw, he could use a little powdering and puffing himself. He'd take a turn in the shower...after he showed Diana what was in his gear bag.

Retreating, Charlie straightened the bedcovers, then dragged his flight suit from the canvas bag and laid it on the downy comforter. His jaw went tight as bits of hardened rubber crumbled onto the spread.

He stared at the dark crumbs for a long moment, then spun on his heel and aimed for the kitchenette to tackle the coffeemaker mounted under the cupboard. When Diana emerged from the mist-filled bathroom wrapped from chin to toe in a thick white terry-cloth robe, he was waiting with a steaming mug and a terse instruction.

"Take a look at the rubber seals and hoses."

Finger-combing her damp hair away from her face, she hitched a hip on the side of the bed to study the full pressure suit. The white bubble helmet and steel gray, one-piece body cover were devoid of all markings. No flag on the sleeve, no rank insignia, nothing to identify the wearer at all.

"It looks just like a space suit."

Charlie shrugged. From the material she'd shown him of the Apollo flights, he guessed NASA had adapted much of the gear tested by early high-altitude pilots.

"Space as a physical environment begins a hundred and twenty-five miles above the earth," he confirmed. "As a physiological environment, it begins at about fifty-five thousand feet."

"And the U-2 could cruise at sixty thousand," she murmured.

"Our pilots faced the same dangers of hypoxia, decompression sickness, Armstrong's Line, and extreme cold as they would in orbit."

Charlie had learned early in the U-2 program that Armstrong's Line was the atmospheric point where water boiled at 98.6—exact body temperature. The pressure suit was designed to protect the U-2 pilots' blood from bubbling and boiling when they reached that altitude. Since outside temperatures could reach seventy degrees below zero, the suit also protected against hypothermia, frostbite and frozen eyeballs in the event the aircraft lost cabin heat.

"The key component of the pressure suit is the integrated breathing system," he explained, his voice grim. "When in flight, the system provides the pilot with one hundred percent oxygen at all times—even during ejection.''

Without a full pressure suit at high elevation, a pilot had only about a minute before the lack of oxygen caused blurred vision, dizziness, slowed reactions and lack of muscle coordination. Charlie had experienced each of those terrifying conditions first-hand.

Scooping up a handful of the granulated pebbles that peppered the bedspread, he dropped them into Diana's palm. ''Those are what I want analyzed.''

Frowning, she rolled the shreds of hardened rubber back and forth in her palm. ''We ran tests on all your gear at the recovery site. None of the tests indicated the possibility of equipment failure.''

''How did you explain those?''

''The rubber components in your equipment froze when you went into the sea, then disintegrated when they were exposed to air again.''

He opened his mouth, snapped it shut again. The terror of his last seconds in flight came rushing back. He could almost hear the deadly hiss of escaping oxygen. Feel his mind start to spin. Like a wild beast, he'd clawed at his helmet, sucking desperately for air before training and pure survival instinct had taken over.

''The rubber started disintegrating in midflight, Diana.''

''What?''

"I lost oxygen at full cruise altitude, just after entering Soviet airspace."

Her fist clenched over the pebbles. "Are you sure?"

"I'm sure." A clammy sweat filmed Charlie's skin. The residue of fear left a metallic bitterness in his mouth. "I jerked the stick and brought the aircraft around. I had her on a westerly trajectory when the oxygen system failed completely and I ejected."

"Dear God!"

"I lost consciousness on the way down. I don't remember my chute deploying or hitting the water. I don't remember *anything* after popping the canopy."

"Why didn't you tell us about this during the recovery operation?"

"At first, because I couldn't believe your incredible story that I'd spent all those years in the ice. Then..."

Gripping the nuggets tight in her fist, Diana pushed off the bed. "Then, Charlie?"

"Then I remembered that we'd tested the effects of superoxygenation during the U-2 shakedown flights. The tests were discontinued when the aircraft went operational—over the strenuous objections of one of the young scientists working the initial program."

"What young scientist?" Her eyes went wide

with shocked comprehension. "Oh, no! Not Dr. Goode?"

"Bingo."

Denial rose swift and hot in Diana's chest. She was a scientist to her bones. She lived and breathed research, discovery, unlocking the secrets of the universe that surrounded her. Irwin Goode had achieved an almost God-like status in her field.

"You can't suspect Dr. Goode of having anything to do with the disintegration of your life support equipment!"

"At this point, I don't suspect anyone of anything. I just want you to run more tests. Without Goode looking over your shoulder this time."

"He's a Nobel Prize winner, Charlie! One of the most respected names in microbiology. His early work laid the foundation for the whole science of bionetics. The United States Army still uses him as one of their primary resources for questions and issues pertaining to biological warfare research, for Pete's sake."

"All I want is to run more tests," he repeated stubbornly.

"But..."

She broke off, her breath hitching. With the resonating clarity of a bell, she heard Dr. Goode's protest that Charlie's cells couldn't possibly be regenerating protein. He himself had calibrated the laser scanning microscope that was supposed to record any level of life-sustaining activity.

The same microscope that had delivered the faulty readings!

Cursing, Diana castigated herself as a dozen kinds of a fool. She'd suspected Greg Wozniak's motives for insisting that Charlie be declared legally dead, had even set OMEGA to digging into the cyrogeneticist's background. But her respect for Irwin Goode had blinded her to the possibility that the venerable biologist might have joined the recovery team with an agenda that didn't include bringing Major Charles Stone back to life.

She didn't like the fact that her personal biases as a scientist had gotten in the way of her job as an undercover operative…any more than she relished the task of digging into Dr. Goode's past.

Heck of a morning this was turning out to be, she thought savagely. First she'd had to face the brutal truth that her performance in bed last night had won Charlie's confidence. Now one of her all-time idols might just tumble right off his pedestal.

At least she could pass on the information that the Russians apparently *hadn't* shot down Charlie's plane. With the president about to depart for Moscow, that news would be welcome. What wouldn't be as welcome was the news that one of the United States's most eminent scientists might have somehow been involved in the crash.

Dammit! This altered everything, including the need for increased levels of security. She'd better contact OMEGA, and fast.

"I need to think about this," she told Charlie. "Why don't I call room service and order us up some breakfast while you hit the shower?"

She waited until she heard the water sandblasting the shower tiles before she whipped up the phone. Room service promised two American-plan breakfasts within twenty minutes.

That gave her twenty minutes to think. Still gripping the hardened bits of rubber, she wandered into the sitting room and out onto the deck. The tide was in, she saw at a glance. The wooden stairs zigzagging down to the beach ended almost at water's edge. Like gleeful girls in white petticoats kicking up their heels, each wave that crashed against the rocks flung up curls of lacy spume.

Her mind racing, Diana considered the options. She could bundle Charlie back to Edwards. The controlled-access air force base would provide a basic level of security while OMEGA ran the tests he'd requested. Or she could keep him here, where no one—including Dr. Goode—knew he was.

With one eye on the bedroom door, Diana punched in the chronometer's knob.

"Go ahead, Artemis."

She might have known Mackenzie would answer.

The woman probably hadn't even gone home last night.

"I've changed my mind, Comm. I need you to get someone out here to run a screen and set up active and passive security systems. I want the best from your bag of tricks," she warned. "Quiet. Undetectable. Infallible."

"Ahhh, I love a personal challenge like that. I'll pull up the layout of the resort and see what protective measures will work best. We should be able set them up today. If I need you out of there, can you and the iceman disappear for an hour or so?"

"No problem. Just let me know when."

"Will do. Anything else?"

"I'd also like for you to arrange a courier. I want some samples hand-delivered to Dr. Sylvie Marquez-Jourdain at the Lawrence Livermore National Lab in Berkeley. I'll call ahead and arrange the specific tests I need run."

"I'll have a courier there within a half hour. Is that it?"

"No." She blew out a breath. "I need to talk to Lightning."

"He left for Paris two hours ago." A faint note of disapproval crept into Mackenzie's voice. "Emmanuelle Béart is dining at Nickz tonight and specifically requested the owner to join her."

"I hate to spoil his dinner with the sexy star of

Mission: Impossible, but you'd better patch me through to his jet.''

"Will do.''

The call went out via a secure device that scrambled each word at the transmission point and unscrambled it at the receiving end. Once the connection was established, Lightning listened intently to Diana's hurried report.

"Well,'' he said after she finished, "at least I can inform the president that Soviets apparently didn't shoot down Major Stone's plane. I have a hard time believing that one of our country's venerable scientists had anything to do with it, though.''

"You and me both!''

"What's the plan now, Artemis?''

"I need you to pull some strings with the CIA. I want copies of any documents relating to Dr. Goode's work with the initial U-2 cadre. Particularly his early experiments in superoxygenation.''

After agreeing to exercise his muscle as OMEGA's new director, Nick concurred with Diana's recommendation that she and Charlie remain in Santa Monica.

"It's as good a spot as any to keep Major Stone under wraps until we sort through all this. Do you need backup?''

"No, I've got it covered. I've asked Comm to install additional security, just in case.''

"Good enough. Keep me posted, Artemis.''

"Will do.''

*   *   *

Diana was in the sitting room nursing a mug of coffee when Charlie emerged from the bathroom, showered and shaved and outfitted in a red knit polo shirt and brand new jeans that looked and felt as though they'd been run through the wringer a couple dozen times. Burying a pang of nostalgia for the stiff-legged, rolled-cuff jeans of his era, he filled a mug and joined her on the plaid sofa.

She'd used his time in the shower to dress as well, exchanging the terry-cloth robe for loose-fitting tan linen slacks with a drawstring waist and a short-sleeved ocean green top. Her still-damp hair framed her face in careless waves. Wedging her back into the corner of the sofa, she curled her legs under her and regarded him through the steam rising from her mug.

"Breakfast should be here any minute. I ordered omelettes for both of us."

"Good. I'm starved."

Charlie hooked an ankle over his knee. The tension that had ridden his back from the moment he'd opened his eyes at the oceanographic station still sat square on his shoulders—it would until he had some answers—but sharing it with Diana had lightened the load exponentially. That, and the incredible pleasure they'd shared last night. Just the thought of how she'd given herself so joyously, so generously, generated a different brand of tension altogether. Smiling at the sensation, he tipped his mug to her.

"I've also contacted a colleague at Lawrence Livermore National Lab," she said, ignoring the invitation buried in his smile. "She's agreed to run a full spectrum of tests on the rubber samples. A courier will be here within the hour to hand-carry the samples to Berkeley."

Charlie didn't alter his lazy sprawl, but her distant tone sent up a whole mast full of red flags. What the heck happened while he was in the shower?

"You've been busy."

"That's me, Dr. Efficiency."

His mug went to the table beside the sofa. Unhooking his ankle, he squared around to face her. "What's going on here, Diana?"

"Exactly what you wanted. Once we get the samples analyzed, we'll decide the next step."

"I'm not talking about the samples."

Her glance flicked over him, as sharp and cutting as slivers of ice. "What are you talking about, then?"

"Us. Last night."

"Last night happened. It was...enjoyable."

Enjoyable? He took the hit right where it hurt most. His pride would have crashed and burned right there if the hard glitter in her eyes hadn't warned him he was missing something vital in this conversation.

"You might be experiencing a few morning-after doubts," he said slowly, "but I'm not. Those hours with you took me higher and faster and farther than I've ever flown in my life."

Diana wanted to believe him. Emotionally, she longed to believe there was no direct cause and effect between the astonishing passion they'd ignited and Charlie's decision to share his secret with her. Intellectually, she couldn't break the connection. She'd crossed the line with him, and now had to pay the price. Scrubbing the heel of her hand across her forehead, she was as honest as she could be in the circumstances.

"All right, I broke a few speed and endurance records last night, too. The problem is we went too far, too fast."

"It's a physical impossibility for a test pilot to go too far *or* too fast, sugar."

She refused to let his swift, slashing grin distract her. "You just spent forty years plus buried in ice. We're not even sure yet why you landed there. Until we get the answers you're looking for, we can't allow physical needs to cloud our thinking or our judgment."

To her surprise, laughter sprang in his eyes.

"Do you find something amusing?" she asked frigidly.

"No! It's just that…"

"What?"

"In my time, that always used to be the guy's line. It generally went something like 'let's not make too big a deal of this, it was just a physical thing, I'll call you.'"

"I'm serious here, Charlie. You've raised some unsettling questions. Until they're answered, we'd better switch to a hands-off mode."

His amusement faded. "Are you upset because I've thrown some doubts on your precious Dr. Goode?"

"Of course not! I'm just suggesting we...we throttle back a little."

"I'm not sure I can turn whatever it is you do to me off and on that easily," he said slowly.

"Try."

For pity's sake! Why was she letting him put her on the defensive like this? Stone was supposed to be the hotshot, love 'em and leave 'em flyboy. He'd probably used that line he rattled off a moment ago dozens of times in his heyday. It was on the tip of Diana's tongue to remind him of those blankets he claimed to have spread under the pier when knuckles rapped against the front door.

"That should be breakfast," she said, assuming a calm she was a long way from feeling. "Do you want to have it here or on the deck?"

The courier arrived while they were still sitting in the sun, tossing the remnants of their toast to the gulls that dive-bombed from dizzying heights to snatch the morsels out of the air. Charlie said nothing when Diana handed over the package she'd carefully wrapped in one of the plastic trash bags they'd found under the counter of the well-equipped kitchenette.

Once the rubber samples were on the way to the lab at Berkeley, the day that had begun amid a tangle of warm sheets stretched cold and empty before them. Restless, Charlie flipped through the TV channels while Diana checked her e-mail and attended to the details of her civilian life. By ten, he'd had his fill of cartoons, morning talk shows, and gloomy stock market predictions. By noon, he was prowling the bungalow.

"I'm going to take a walk on the beach."

Diana flipped down the computer's screen. "I'll come with you."

"Suit yourself."

His shrug told her he hadn't worked his way past the screeching halt she'd put on their physical activities. Neither had she, for that matter.

It was the right decision, she echoed silently, repeatedly, as they tracked footprints through the sand. The only decision.

She was still trying to convince herself over a late lunch, eaten at an open-air fish restaurant a mile or so down the beach, and later, when they trudged back to the resort. They climbed the wooden stairs to the bungalow, tired and wind-burned and still edgy with each other. So edgy, Diana almost missed the glint of sunlight on steel just inside the sliding glass doors.

She caught a glimpse of it when Charlie snapped the door back on its runners. Only a glimpse.

That was all she needed. She recognized the business end of a gun barrel when she saw it. Leaping across the weathered planks, she made a grab for Charlie. To her consternation, he hooked her arm, spun her behind him, and lunged through the door.

Chapter 10

"Charlie, wait!"

Diana's frantic shout went unheeded as Charlie plunged through the open door. Recovering her balance, she exploded into the bedroom after him.

Every instinct she possessed screamed that this was exactly the wrong move. The first rule of protective services was to keep the client safe, to hustle him or her away at any hint of danger. That was why ex-cops and military types made such bad bodyguards! They were trained to attack, or at the very least neutralize the threat.

Which was obviously Charlie's plan.

With a snarling curse, he launched himself at the man crouched over the open canvas gear bag, a pistol gripped in one plastic-gloved hand. The intruder sprang up, shot a dismayed look at Diana over Charlie's flying form, and took the body block square in his chest. Staggering back, he crashed into the wall behind him and went down, taking his attacker with him. A bone-cracking chop to his wrist sent his weapon sailing through the air.

Oh, Lord!

To a chorus of grunts and thuds, Diana scrambled over the gear that had been dumped out of the canvas bag onto the carpet. She had to disengage Charlie before he inflicted serious bodily injury.

"What in the world...?"

The sound of running footsteps brought Diana whirling around. She speared a single glance at the startled woman in a blue-gray body suit and turned her attention back to the two combatants.

OMEGA's chief of communications took in the scene and swore. Lightning wasn't going to like this! With that thought going off like a klaxon in Mackenzie's head, she dumped the tangle of wires in her hand and waded into the fray beside Diana.

They both made a grab for the arm Major Stone swung back in a vicious arc, but before either could get a firm grip, he smashed his fist into the other man's jaw.

Poor John, Mackenzie thought ruefully. His head snapped back. His eyeballs rolled. With a soft little gurgle, he went limp.

Chest heaving, the Iceman straddled his unconscious opponent and studied him for signs of life, which gave Mackenzie a few tense seconds to study *him*. Sand still clumped on the soles of his bare feet. His red polo shirt gaped at the neck, half the buttons ripped away. The muscles under the red knit remained coiled and ready to spring. Mackenzie formed the impression of a distinctly lethal male.

Sitting back on his heels, Stone raked her with a hard glance. She could imagine how she must look with her black hair falling from its loose bun, her headphones draped around her neck and antistatic booties tied over her sneakers.

"Who the hell are you?"

Several possible answers formed instantly in her mind. Rather than rattle one off, Mackenzie looked to the woman beside her for a cue. This was her show, after all.

Diana hesitated, then dipped her head in a slow nod. "Tell him."

Relief coursed through Mackenzie. Despite the pummeling he'd just given her assistant, Major Stone was one of the good guys. He'd gone through enough without confusing him even more with some hastily concocted tale. Besides, whatever she came up with to explain her presence and the equipment scattered through the bungalow would sound lame...even to a man who'd been out of action as long as Charlie Stone.

"I'm chief of communications for a government agency."

"What agency?"

"It's highly classified," Mackenzie began, but Stone wasn't about to be palmed off with such a convenient excuse.

"Don't give me that bull! What agency?"

Calmly, Diana deflected his aim. "The same one I work for."

Stone's incredible baby-blues knifed into the woman beside Mackenzie. Suspicion flared hot in his eyes, before icing over almost instantly. "You told me you work for a private research institute."

"I do. I also take on certain special…assignments…when directed or requested."

His face went hard and tight. Pushing to his feet, he advanced on the two women. Diana stood her ground. Mackenzie did the same, although she wasn't above admitting to a distinct qualm. Up close and personal, the Iceman presented a rather large and very muscular target.

"You want to tell me just what your *assignment* is here?"

The serrated edge to his voice could have sawed right through an anchor cable.

"I was detailed to act as a combination body-guard and handler."

That went down about as easily as the highly classified bit had. A muscle ticked in Stone's left cheek. His eyes turned glacial. Mackenzie didn't require any special communications skills to get the message. The major didn't particularly appreciate being guarded *or* handled.

"I'll give you full marks for dedication to your job," he said, skewering Diana with a look that could have stripped paint from a ship's bulwark. "In my day, jumping into the sack with an *assignment* would have been considered above and beyond the call of duty. Guess the rules have changed."

Red surged into Diana's cheeks. Her mouth opened, snapped shut. After an obvious mental ten-count, she tried again.

"Why don't we continue this conversation in the other room? I'll join you there as soon as Comm and I make sure her tech's okay."

Rubbing his bruised knuckles, Stone flicked the man on the floor an unsympathetic glance, then stalked across the room to retrieve the weapon he'd sent flying a few moments ago. With a precision that left no doubt about the ownership of the long-barreled Colt, he released the safety, flipped open the cylinder to check for a chambered round, and snapped it closed again. Both he and the Colt disappeared into the other room a moment later.

"Whew!" Blowing out a long breath, Mackenzie turned to her friend. "Sorry about this, Artemis."

"It's okay. I didn't expect to see you here, Comm."

"I hopped a plane right after you called." Her mouth twisted. "I should've let you know we were on-site. Since you weren't here when we arrived, we just slipped in and went to work."

"We took a walk down the beach."

"I know. We were tracking you via the transponder in your watch. We planned to be out of here before you and the Iceman headed back this way. The electronic screens we set up must have scrambled your transponder's signals."

With a mental note to adjust the electromagnetic pulse the screens emitted, Mackenzie dropped down on one knee and eased her now groaning tech into a sitting position.

"Anything broken or otherwise dented?"

John worked his jaw from side to side to the accompaniment of a few bone-cracking pops.

"Just my pride," he admitted.

Middle-aged, happily married and the father of four, he'd worked for OMEGA for years. To anyone's knowledge, this was the first time he'd ever been taken down on a job.

With Diana's assistance, Mackenzie helped him to his feet. "What happened?"

"When I tested the bedroom sensors, they recorded the presence of cordite. I had just tracked it to the handgun in Major Stone's gear bag when he and Artemis returned. The situation, uh, deteriorated at that point."

"No kidding."

Her ready grin eased his embarrassment almost as much as her assurance that he'd followed correct operating procedures. The inventory of Major Stone's gear Artemis had sent back from the oceanographic station had listed the Colt, but John was right to check it out anyway. Only a fool would rig electronic devices without verifying the source and amount of gunpowder or explosive materials present at the work site.

"Major Stone saw the Colt in your hand," Diana explained. "He shoved me out of the line of fire and launched his attack before I could stop him."

"Oh, that's good." Mackenzie's grin widened. "The iceman was trying to protect you. No wonder he looked so surprised when he learned you were here to protect *him*."

Surprised and not particularly thrilled.

Mackenzie didn't know Stone well enough to assess his male ego, but her ex had sported one the size of Texas. Too handsome for his own or anyone else's good, the jerk had charmed her into the mistaken notion that she'd formed the only bright, shining star in his solar system. He'd also honestly believed that his career took precedence over hers. After all, the military was a man's world, and Ensign Blair had a husband only too willing to take care of her.

Unfortunately, too many senior officers in command positions subscribed to the same mentality. Mackenzie had butted against their paternalistic attitudes for far longer than she should have, but had finally left both Lieutenant Commander Blair *and* the navy behind.

Thank goodness OMEGA's former director had recruited her to take over as communications chief just days after she'd hung up her uniform. Mackenzie would always be grateful to Maggie Sinclair. Since joining the agency, she hadn't had time to regret either her career switch or her divorce. Much.

"Let's finish up and get the heck out of Dodge," she instructed John. "Artemis needs to soothe the Iceman's ruffled feathers. And what fine feathers they are," she added, sending a sideways glance at the man in the other room as John went back to work.

Although Mackenzie didn't regret shedding her ex, she did occasionally mourn lack of anything remotely resembling libidinous activity in her life. If only there was some way to filter out their annoying little quirks, men would definitely have a few uses.

"You were right about one thing," she murmured to Diana. "The Iceman's in incredible physical condition. No wonder you decided to, er, maintain positive surveillance last night."

"Last night was a mistake."

The total lack of inflection in her friend's voice spoke volumes.

"Oh, no! You're not going to tell me Major Stone forgot how to use all that glorious man-muscle those forty years he was asleep, are you?"

"No, but *I* forgot a few pertinent issues. For one thing, the man's just come out of a semi-permanent deep freeze. For another, he hadn't yet decided he could trust me with this business about his flight gear." She hesitated, then lifted her shoulders in a shrug that didn't quite disguise her anger and self-disgust. "Evidently I convinced him with my performance in bed."

"Ouch!"

"Yeah," Diana bit out. "Ouch."

The communications team finished rigging both active and passive defenses twenty minutes later.

"The passive systems are mostly for intrusion detection," Mackenzie informed Diana and the major. "We've set up infrared sensors that will activate a silent alarm."

Pointing to what looked like an ordinary light switch, she explained how the system worked. "When tripped by someone approaching the unit, the alarm sends a pulsing vibration through the sitting room, the bedroom, and the bathroom. You turn it on and off with this switch to allow access by maids, room service, whoever. John, go outside and activate the sensors so they can feel the pulse."

The rippling sensation that traveled up Diana's

bare arms a few moments later felt like a gentle whirlpool, without the warm water.

"We've also placed eight high resolution cameras in strategic positions inside and outside the cottage." Picking up the TV remote, Mackenzie demonstrated the visual sweep. "You hit channel sixty-one to run through all eight cameras, channel sixty-two to freeze at a particular location."

A single click of the remote brought images of astonishing color and clarity to life. Like tulips opening and closing their petals, they faded on and off the screen in five-second intervals. There was the crushed shell path bordered in brilliant scarlet hibiscus. The Golden Hawk sitting in solitary splendor in the small parking space. The weathered teakwood deck suspended high over the dazzling Pacific. The chintz-filled sitting room. The king-sized bed.

Remembering all too vividly what had occurred in that bed scant hours ago, Diana asked for quick clarification. "Do the surveillance cameras feed only to this TV?"

"This one and the one in the bedroom. They also transmit digital signals by satellite to the control center." Mackenzie assumed a carefully neutral expression. "If at any time you require privacy, you can interrupt the signals. Just hit channel 62."

"Right."

"Now for the active defenses…"

Charlie kept his back propped against the wall and his arms crossed as the long-legged brunette with the tangle of wires draped around her neck went on to demonstrate a grab bag of defenses. Each was strategically placed to stun, temporarily blind, or otherwise incapacitate any uninvited and un-wanted guests.

With each passing moment, he felt more and more like he'd stepped right onto the set of a science fiction movie. Godzilla meets the Martian Invaders. Although he had to admit the ray guns and space ships in the grainy, black-and-white horror films that used to scare the dickens out of moviegoers in his day couldn't hold a candle to this stuff!

Pulsing waves. Infrared beams. Ultrahigh frequency, directed-energy nerve blockers. Holy cow!

The brunette had blithely assured Diana and Charlie that she'd fed their bio-signatures into the profile cache—whatever the hell that was. Supposedly, their movements inside the cottage wouldn't trigger the lasers and nerve guns. Even if Charlie had understood one word in every three she tossed out, her airy assurances would have done little to ease the anger coiled around his gut.

He was a test pilot. He'd defied gravity, beat all the odds. Wrung the kinks out of the most advanced aircraft of his day, for God's sake! Yet the suppos-edly sophisticated systems that drove his planes were crude and primitive compared to this space-aged technology.

That alone was enough to twist him into knots…if Diana's revelation that she'd been *assigned* to protect him hadn't already done the trick.

Charlie wasn't a fool. He respected talent and ability when he saw it. More to the point, he'd come to manhood during a war that had convulsed the whole world, a war in which ordinary men *and* women were called upon to perform the most extraordinary deeds. Women's Air Service Pilots had ferried every aircraft in the U.S. inventory across the Atlantic to the Allies, often without fighter escort. American WACs and WAVEs served in every theater of the war. Female aces like the White Rose of Russia had racked up an impressive number of kills in defense of the Motherland. And later, during the Korean conflict, nurses had served under the most unimaginable conditions at or near the front.

But none of the women who'd served during these conflicts had been ordered to take the offensive. Or climbed into the cockpit of a fighter to fly cover for their male counterparts. Knowing this shadowy agency Diana worked for had sent her to do just that blasted Charlie's ingrained, inbred notions about the role of the sexes all to hell. Knowing she'd played him like a cheap violin didn't go down any easier, either.

"That's it," the curvaceous brunette said after a

final demo. "Oh, except for the material you requested on the early U-2 cadre. The chief wrangled access to CIA's archives, but they've been dragging their feet producing the reports we requested. I'll e-mail them to you as soon as they release them."

"Thanks."

With a nod to Charlie, the brunette and her assistant hefted their handy-dandy, whiz-bang tool kits and departed the premises.

Diana saw them out, then bent one leg under her and plopped down on the sofa. Her linen slacks made a pale pool against the splashy plaid. Wind and salt spray had pinked her nose and churned her hair into a wild tangle, but she didn't appear particularly bothered by either. Charlie made no move to break the silence that spun out between them. This was her show. Let her do the explaining.

To his disgust, she didn't attempt to explain a damned thing. In a cool voice that scraped along his nerves like nails on a chalkboard, she simply stated her case.

"The fact that I work for the government doesn't change anything."

"The fact that you didn't bother to tell me you work for the government changes everything."

"How?"

"How do you think? I take off on a mission and wake up forty-five years later. From the first moment I opened my eyes, you were right there, offering your friendship, holding my hand, leaving me so hungry for you I could hardly walk upright. Through it all, you neglect to mention that you're just following orders.''

Her chin tipped. ''We'd better get one thing straight, right here, right now. My orders do not include having sex with you.''

The blunt reply poured oil on the fire already smoldering in Charlie's gut. Is that how she categorized what happened last night? They'd had sex? He might have used similar terms in a locker room when joking around with the guys, but not with a woman. And definitely not with Diana.

There was no way he would classify their joining as mere sex. Diana Remington had turned him inside out. He'd never made love with anyone so open, so eager. He could almost hear her gasp, feel her muscles tightening around his aching shaft as she spasmed with pleasure.

They might have been driven by mindless lust the first time. Maybe even the second. But by the third, her movements had become as slow and languorous as his, her groans deep and wrenching. Diana couldn't have prevented that last, volcanic explosion if she'd wanted to, any more than he could have kept from digging his hands in her hair, tipping her head back, and claiming her mouth at the same time he emptied himself into her body.

Both mollified and irritatingly, instantly aroused

by the memory of how she'd all but come apart in his arms, he rapped out a curt request. "Maybe you'd better tell me just what your orders do include."

She looked him straight in the eye. "To get close to you and gain your confidence. Ultimately, to find out what happened to you and your aircraft all those years ago."

She didn't pull any punches, he'd give her that. Despite his simmering anger, Charlie found himself wanting to believe her.

"The president needed to know if the Soviets shot your plane down, as they did Gary Powers's in 1960," she said coolly. "He hoped to avoid another international outcry over U.S. spy planes violating other nation's airspace, like the one that occurred after the Powers incident. At the same time, he was worried that certain ultra right-wing radical groups in the United States could use you as a rallying point to revive the Cold War. There's still a lot of anti-Soviet sentiment left over from those days."

Those days. Suddenly, Charlie felt as though he'd stepped right out of an ancient history book. And to tell the truth, he still harbored one heck of a case of anti-Soviet sentiment. He couldn't get his mind around the notion that they weren't the bad guys any more.

"Well, you accomplished half your mission," he remarked sardonically. "We still don't know what happened to my aircraft, but you certainly got close to me.''

"Yes," she agreed with a shrug, "I passed the test.''

"What test?''

She looked away, but not before he caught the spark of anger darkening her eyes. Where the heck did that come from? He was the one who'd been played like a fish.

"What test?'' he asked again.

She glanced back, her expression now carefully bland. "Look, it's okay. Evidently we both got our signals crossed. You thought I seduced you on orders, and I thought you wanted me as much as I wanted you. I only realized this morning that having sex constituted the final test before you decided you could trust me enough to..."

"That's the biggest bunch of crap I've heard in forty-five years!''

Stiffening, she sent him an icy glare. "I beg your pardon?''

"What we did last night went beyond mere sex, and you damned well know it.'' Shoving away from the wall, Charlie stalked across the gray carpet. "As for wanting you...''

If he hadn't been so riled...

If she hadn't thrown him for a loop with the business of working for the government...

If his whole blasted world hadn't turned upside

down, he might not have used quite so much force when he wrapped his fingers around her wrist and yanked her off the sofa.

Two seconds later, he was flat on his back.

Chapter 11

Charlie hit the carpet butt-first.

Diana hadn't intended to take him down. She certainly hadn't planned to reverse his hold on her wrist, duck under his arm and flip him head over heels. She simply reacted to his aggression and her own banked anger.

"I told you before," she reminded him coolly, "these kind of caveman tactics went out with the poodle skirt."

She had a moment, a mere moment, to savor the look of owlish surprise on his face before his hand whipped out and knocked her feet out from under her.

She could have broken her fall, could have gone

into a tuck and roll and regained her feet before he scrambled to his, but she figured one hundred and twenty plus pounds of deadweight landing square on Charlie's midsection might get his attention once and for all.

Her calculations failed to take into consideration reflexes honed by years in the cockpit of high-performance test aircraft. She was still on her way down when Charlie sucked in a swift breath, contracted his stomach muscles, and hardened her designated landing site. Diana's bottom bounced off what felt like a solid concrete slab. The next instant, she was flat on *her* back.

"Watch it, buster," she warned when he straddled her thighs and pinned her wrists to the gray plush. "I don't want to hurt you."

"Think you could?"

"Given your present position, my knee has the potential to become a lethal weapon."

To Diana's considerable relief, he relaxed his grip on her wrists. She really *didn't* want to hurt him. He neglected, however, to remove his weight from her thighs. Planting his palms on the floor beside her head, he tossed her earlier words right back at her.

"We'd better get one thing straight, right here, right now, Remington. I didn't take you to bed last night as some kind of perverted test."

"Really? Then maybe you'll explain why you

waited until this morning to tell me that your flight suit disintegrated in midair.''

"I planned to tell you yesterday, when we left Harry's house, but needed to think a few things through. Then, after we got here, other matters took priority.''

Which was a polite way of saying the front door had barely closed behind them before they'd ended up on the carpet only a few feet from where they now sprawled.

"I wanted you so badly," he admitted, "I could hardly walk straight, let alone think straight. Last night, my number one goal was to get you naked and horizontal.''

Well, that was honest enough! Diana thought about admitting she been driven by exactly the same goal, but settled for a small shrug.

"All right, maybe I wasn't thinking very straight last night, either. This morning's a different story, Charlie.''

The tension that had snapped and cracked between them eased. So did the weight pinning her thighs to the carpet. Squirming upright, Diana tucked her knees under her. He waited until she'd gotten comfortable to pick up the knotty thread of their conversation.

"So that's why you decided we should switch to hands-off mode this morning? You thought I'd told you about the disintegration of my flight gear as a bonus for your performance in bed last night?''

She grimaced at the phrasing, but couldn't deny that was exactly what she'd thought. ''Yes, in part.''

''What's the other part?''

''I also honestly believe we should slow down. We've let this…this attraction between us heat up to the flash point. We need to cool off, give you time to find your balance again before…''

''Before you toss me on my head?'' he cut in dryly.

There was no way Diana intended to apologize for that. ''I got your attention, didn't I?''

''Yeah, you did.'' He leveled a long, considering look at her. ''You're good at this spy business, aren't you?''

She wasn't going to apologize for that, either. ''We prefer to call it undercover operations these days, and yes, I am. If you have a problem with what I do, Charlie, I suggest you get over it.''

He snapped his fingers. ''Just like that?''

''Just like that.''

Her clear green eyes held his. Their challenge was unmistakable. Charlie nursed his bruised pride, trying to work past the idea that Diana had been assigned to protect him, when everything in him said it should be the other way around. It would take some doing, but he'd give it his best shot.

''I'll tell you what. I'll try to stop acting like a

fifties jerk if you stop pretending we can put the brakes on this attraction, as you call it, between us.''

"Charlie, listen to me…''

"No, you listen for a change. I told you this morning, I can't flip whatever it is I'm feeling for you on and off like a light switch.''

"That's just the problem! You don't know what you're feeling. Neither do I.''

"I know it's more than just sex, Diana.''

He waited with a show of deliberate patience.

"All right, it's more than just sex.''

Thrusting her fingers through her hair, she shot him a helpless glance. The fact that she couldn't flip her feelings on and off, either, acted like a balm to his lacerated pride. His anger fizzled, not dying completely, but losing enough of its heat for him to listen patiently while she ran through a litany of arguments.

"I was the first person you saw when you woke up. I was also the one who broke the news that you'd skipped a few years of your life. And you… You became a personal challenge, Charlie. I lost my scientific objectivity somewhere around my second or third day at the recovery site. Despite the readings, despite the lack of protein generation, I refused to give up on you. It's natural that we should develop a…a bond.''

"You think so?''

"I know so.''

"I've got news for you, babe. When I woke up and you fed me the crazy story about being on ice all those years, my first thought was that you were part of some crazy Commie plot. I was sure you were trying to scramble my brain."

"But once you got past that?"

He thought of a half-dozen quick comebacks, but none of them made it past his lips. Instead, he found himself uttering the plain, unvarnished truth.

"By the time I got past that, I was already hooked."

The fight went out of her. Her mouth closed, opened. A ragged murmur escaped.

"Oh, boy."

"Yeah. Oh, boy."

Lifting his hands, he cupped her face. His thumb grazed a slow path along her lower lip.

"You're right in one respect, Remington. I did latch onto you. You became my lifeline, a beacon to guide me through an uncharted sea. Even when I wasn't sure I could trust you, I held on for dear life."

His thumb made another slow pass. Diana's breath caught as he bent and grazed her lips with his own. When he raised his head again, his rueful half smile started an ache in her heart.

"I'm not sure I could let go now if I wanted to."

She almost melted on the spot. Only the counter-arguments churning in her mind kept her from flinging her arms around his neck and taking him down once again.

"Oh, Charlie, don't you see? What you're experiencing could be classified as an intense situational dependency. The same emotional dependency hostages sometimes feel for their kidnappers."

A smile lit his eyes. "Come on, blondie. Do you really think I can't tell the difference between desperation and desire?"

"No. Yes. Oh, I don't know!" Thrown off kilter, she tried again. "You haven't had time to find your feet in the twenty-first century, much less find another woman to share your days—and your nights—with."

"That's true," he agreed. "But you have to give me a little credit here. I've been around the block enough times to know I don't want another woman. What I don't know is how you feel about this... What did you call it? This intense situation."

He'd tossed the ball right back into her court, darn it. Maybe he was right. Instead of trying to analyze his feelings, it was time she took a hard look at her own.

"I'm on the same runaway roller you are," she admitted slowly. "I keep plunging into doubt and uncertainty, then climbing to dizzying heights of lust and longing and..."

And love?

No! This crazy jumble of emotions couldn't be love.

Could it?

He must have read the question in her eyes. His smile became a swift, rakish grin. "Helluva ride, isn't it?"

"Yes!"

"Well, since there's no jumping off a roller coaster in midcourse, we might as well enjoy the ups and downs."

Bending, he planted another kiss on her mouth. There was nothing tender about this one, nothing gentle. It was hard and hungry and all consuming. Diana was about to go under for the final time when Charlie dragged his head up and swept the room with a frustrated glare.

"Did your friend activate her hidden cameras before she left?"

Oh, Lord! She'd forgotten all about the blasted things. Nothing like providing a first-class peep show for the folks back at OMEGA. If any of the other operatives happened to be in the control center, she'd never live this down.

"They're on," she confirmed.

"I'll take care of them. Channel 62 for privacy, right?"

"Right."

He got a knee under him and pushed to his feet.

Or tried to. Halfway up, he grunted. His entire body went taut.

"Charlie?"

Thinking that he'd spotted something that caught his attention, Diana scrambled to her knees and threw a quick look over her shoulder. She whipped back around just as he toppled over and landed on his butt for the second time in less than twenty minutes.

Tight white lines etched into either side of his mouth. Beads of perspiration popped out his forehead. Alarmed, she laid a hand on his cheek. The skin felt cold and clammy against her palm.

"Charlie, what's the matter?"

As quickly as it had come, the glazed look in his eyes disappeared.

"Guess I hit the floor harder than I thought a few moments ago," he said slowly.

Guilt swamped Diana until she remembered how he'd stumbled while they were dancing at the pier last night. White lines had cut into his cheeks then, too, but he'd shrugged off the incident. So had she.

Cursing herself for a fool, she snatched up his wrist and searched for his pulse. It galloped under her fingertips for a few seconds before gradually slowing.

"You'd better sit here and rest a little while."

"I'm all right," he insisted, pushing to his feet.

He made it all the way up this time. Jumping up, Diana planted herself right in front of him.

"Don't go all tough and he-man on me, mister. Something's wrong and we need to find out what. How many of these dizzy spells have you had?"

"Three or four."

"Why didn't you tell the flight surgeon at Edwards about them?"

"Because I didn't attach any particular significance to them."

She gave a little puff of disgust.

"Occasional dizziness is an occupational hazard that comes with flying the U-2," he said patiently. "Heat builds up in the flight suit during taxi, pattern work and landing. Once in flight, you're encased in rubber for nine hours plus at a stretch. I don't know a single U-2 pilot who wasn't a little dizzy and swimming in his own sweat when he finally climbed out of the cockpit."

"You're not wearing a flight suit now," she pointed out with a touch of acid.

"True, but forty plus years on ice could have generated all kinds of delayed reactions."

She didn't have an argument for that.

"I was confused and disoriented for days after I woke up," he offered in further self-defense. "If I experienced any black moments then, they got lost in the shuffle. The first time I really felt the punch was at the pier."

Chewing on her lower lip, Diana weighed the options. Her first impulse was to bundle Charlie into the Hawk, speed back to Edwards, and have the docs take another look at him. Her second, to get on the horn and find out why the flight surgeon hadn't e-mailed her the results of the first battery of tests as promised.

When presented with both options, Charlie voted for the second. ''Might as well see what the tests show before we jump the gun.''

Nodding, she headed for the bedroom in search of the purse she'd dropped when she'd dived through the sliding glass doors after Charlie. She found it on the floor and dug out the flight surgeon's business card. After a quick check of her notebook computer to make sure the information hadn't come in while they'd walked the beach, she put in a call to Edwards. She didn't have to worry about using the regular phone line. Mackenzie had made sure any calls originating from their unit wouldn't be intercepted.

''I'm sorry, ma'am,'' a harried-sounding med tech replied. ''The doctor's with a patient. If you'll leave your number, I'll have him get back to you.''

Frustrated, Diana rattled off the number of the resort. ''Tell him I need to know the test results on Major Stone ASAP.''

''Yes, ma'am.''

* * *

The flight surgeon returned her call twenty minutes later and apologized for not sending the results earlier.

"There was an anomaly in the major's blood work, so I had the lab rerun the tests."

Diana's fingers tightened on the phone. "What kind of anomaly?"

"One of the blood gas samples showed a spike in the oxygen level, yet the other samples all fell within the normal range. Seemed strange, so I decided to check it out. I just got the report back a few minutes ago. Hang on while I skim through it."

Tension crawled up Diana's neck. Toe tapping against the carpet, she clutched the phone in a sweat-dampened palm and counted the seconds.

"Well, this confirms the first test," the doc said a few moments later. "Major Stone's pO2 levels showed significant elevation for that one sample, but not the others."

"How significant?"

"Enough to affect his capillary density. They'd have to contract to counter the increased oxygen flow to his brain."

"Would that cause him to pass out?"

"It could. Why?" the doc asked sharply. "Has he blacked out?"

"No, but he's experienced brief periods of dizziness."

"Well, I don't see any real cause for alarm at this

point, but I'd like to overnight this lab report and the blood samples to a buddy of mine stationed at Brooks Air Force Base in San Antonio.''

Brooks housed the air force's medical research center, Diana knew, a world-renowned center of excellence. Belatedly, she remembered that Dr. Goode had recommended taking Charlie back to Brooks in the first place.

''Lieutenant Colonel Murphy's our foremost expert on the effects of altitude on oxygenation. He's practically written the book on controlling body gasses during the aeromedical transport of critically ill or injured patients. If anyone can make sense of this spike, Murph can.''

''All right, but ask him to get back to you as soon as possible, would you?''

''Sure thing.''

Diana hung up, uneasy and dissatisfied. There were still too many questions, too few answers. A quick glance at her watch showed it was just past three in the afternoon. The courier should have delivered the rubber samples to the Lawrence Livermore Lab by now, but the tests she'd requested would take some hours. It wouldn't hurt to hurry them along a little bit, though.

Moments later, she reached Dr. Sylvie Marquez-Jourdain, formerly Dr. Sylvie Dalton-O'Neil. Diana and Sylvie had shared a microscope their second year of college before opting for different specialties. They'd kept in touch through grad school, Sylvie's three marriages, and Diana's erratic career moves.

"Hey, girl," Sylvie boomed. Larger than life and totally content with her two hundred plus pounds, the biochemist took no prisoners. "I got your package. My folks are slicing and dicing the rubber pellets now. Anything special you want us to look for?"

"No. I just need to know what caused the rubber to crumble into bits like that. And I need it fast, Syl."

"When's the last time you needed something slow?" her friend drawled. Having helped Diana unravel the mystery of a paint solvent that poisoned a high-level diplomat some years ago, she was one of only two people outside OMEGA who knew about Diana's alter ego. The other was Major Charles Stone.

"Just call me as soon as you have something, okay?"

"I will, I will."

After that, there was nothing to do but wait.

Charlie proved better at it than Diana. Restless and worried about his physical condition, she killed some time by rinsing out her slacks and top, which had stiffened from salt spray during their earlier walk. Hanging the wet clothes over the shower rod, she emerged from the bedroom wearing the last of the outfits she'd purchased during the hurried stop at the mall. The gray cotton tunic and leggings were whisper thin and snuggly soft, perfect for warding off the breeze that blew in from the sea.

Charlie's gaze zinged right to the slope of her shoulder, bared by the wide, comfortable tunic neck. She knew him well enough by now to know the appreciation that sprang into his blue eyes had as much to do with the absence of a bra as with the casual but elegant drape of the tunic.

He knew *her* well enough by now to refrain from any comment other than to advise her that he'd ordered dinner from room service.

"Guess we'll see how well all those security gizmos work when it's delivered."

The gizmos worked perfectly. The outside sensors sounded a silent alert. The cameras tracked the arrival of the small entourage with a wheeled cart.

They ate on the deck, witnesses to another glorious sunset. With the sky ablaze in red and gold, Charlie polished off his sea bass. Whatever caused his dizziness certainly hadn't affected his appetite, Diana noted while she picked at her red snapper almondine.

"Not hungry?"

"Not very." She eyed his empty plate. "You did pretty good, all things considered."

"U-2 drivers learn fast never to pass up a meal.

Sometimes we'd go ten, twelve hours between feedings.''

"Tell me," she urged, laying aside her fork. "Talk me through one of your missions."

He hesitated, reluctant even now to reveal exact details of an operation he'd sworn to keep secret. Diana could only begin to appreciate the giant mental leap it required for him to open up.

"Getting ready for a flight took almost as long as the flight itself," he said finally. "We'd conduct all the usual preflight planning, study weather patterns, take intelligence briefs. Then, when we reported to the Life Support, we'd strip down and begin suiting up."

"I read that you weren't allowed to carry any ID or tags that might have identified you as Americans."

"They even snipped the labels off our skivvies."

"I'm sure that completely fooled the Soviets when Powers went down," Diana said solemnly.

"Hey, tell it to the CIA."

"Those amateurs," she sniffed. "Go on."

"Once we were suited up, we spent an hour sitting on our hands while one hundred percent oxygen was pumped through our life support equipment."

"To acclimate you to the pure oxygen that would come through the breathing apparatus in flight?"

"Right. I always hated that idle hour, but knew it was necessary to keep from getting the bends."

The bends!

Diana shot straight up in her chair. With an almost audible click, her mind began to spin frantically.

From the brutal underwater escape and evasion training OMEGA put its agents through, she knew all too well the rapid reduction in surrounding pressure could cause nitrogen bubbles to form in the blood. These bubbles…or beads, as they were called in the diving community…led to decompression sickness, a potentially fatal condition.

But in its more benign state, nitrogen gas comprised seventy-eight percent of the earth's atmosphere. All living things required N2 to live. A relatively stable gas, it was composed of two atoms held together by a tough triple bond. Once broken down, these atoms formed the "amino" in amino acids—the major component in DNA, RNA and proteins.

Breaking down the bond was the key. That only occurred at extremely high temperatures. Or through the magic of nitrogen-fixing bacteria.

Suddenly, all the pieces of the puzzle clicked into place. The faulty readings on the laser scanning microscope Dr. Goode had ordered flown up to the Arctic. The sluggish protein regeneration in Charlie's blood cells. His dizziness. Even the inexplicable oxygen spike.

Damn! The answer had been right in front of her the whole time and she hadn't seen it.

"I've got to call my friend at Lawrence Livermore!"

Bolting out of her chair, she dashed for the phone.

Chapter 12

"Sylvie, this is Diana. Have you...?"

"It was a bacterium," her friend broke in triumphantly. "A rare variant of the nitrogen-fixing microbial consortia. I found traces of several in the samples you sent."

"I knew it!"

There was a ponderous silence at the other end of the line. Sylvie broke it with a disgusted huff.

"Well, hell, girl. If you knew what I was supposed to be looking for, you could have told me up front and saved me all these hours at the lab."

"I just figured it out ten seconds ago, Syl. Listen, you said this was a rare variant. How rare is rare?"

"It's a mutant, actually. Best I recall, this strain

was originally developed as part of an experimental attempt to speed conversion of nitrogen gas to ammonia.''

"Thus boosting the manufacture of amino acids and proteins in living organisms," Diana murmured.

"Exactly."

"Do you know who developed it?" She had an idea, but asked the question anyway.

"I'd have to research the little critter before I give you a definitive answer, but I think it was developed in a lab right here in California. I remember reading that the U.S. Army appropriated it for use in their early biological warfare studies."

The sick certainty that Charlie had been right formed in the pit of Diana's stomach. Dr. Goode's early work had contributed heavily to the army's biological warfare program. And he'd retained an adjunct professorship at UCLA during the years he worked with the U-2 cadre.

She *had* to get access to those CIA files! With a wrench, she tuned back in to what Sylvie was saying.

"This little stinker proved too volatile even for the germ warfare guys. It wreaked havoc on blood gasses of living organisms, but the effect was transitory. Too transitory to make it an effective weapon, anyway."

Bingo! That explained the sporadic spikes in Charlie's blood oxygenation levels. The mutant microbes he'd breathed in during his last flight were still in his blood. Like Charlie, they'd gone to sleep when his blood circulation ceased and his body froze. Now, they'd come alive again.

"What's this variant's life cycle?" she asked urgently.

Most of the common bacteria she was familiar with lived anywhere from two hours to two weeks. There was no telling how long this mutant could exist.

"About twelve days, as I recall, but let me check it out and get back to you."

Diana hung up a moment later, her heart thumping like a brassbound kettledrum. Twelve days. How many days had passed since Charlie woke up? She did a frantic mental count and came up two days short.

Oh, God! What if this microbe was just coming to full strength? What if it sucked in nitrogen from the air and caused beads to form in Charlie's blood? What if he got the bends, died right in front of her!

"What was that all about?"

Whirling, she faced the man standing at her shoulder. The fear that seared through her in a single, blinding flash triggered an instantaneous chain reaction.

The scientist in her acknowledged that she'd lost all detachment where Major Charles Stone was concerned.

The woman in her acknowledged that whatever she felt for him had slipped the point of lust and flirted perilously close to a fierce, desperate love.

Only the undercover agent retained any semblance of control over her emotions. Hanging on to her cool by her fingernails, Diana answered as calmly as she could.

"We know what ate through the rubber seals on your pressure suit...and what's causing your dizzy spells."

He lifted a quizzical brow. "Something tells me I'm not going to like what I'm about to hear."

"It's a bug. A mutant microbe."

"I was right. I don't like it."

"I don't like it much, either."

Using layman's terms whenever possible, Diana recounted what Sylvie had uncovered so far. Luckily, Charlie's training and experience as a high-altitude pilot gave him a ready grasp of the dynamics of atmospheric gasses.

"I don't know why we didn't pick up any sign of this bacterium in the serology samples we took at the oceanographic station." Gnawing on her lower lip, Diana sorted through the possibilities. "It might have been dormant. Or maybe stored in certain root cells, like the shingles virus. My best guess is it only became active after you regained full circulatory function. I'll bet it shows up in the blood sample the flight surgeon at Edwards sent down to

Books, though. In any case, we'd better get you back to the base so we can track this sucker.''

She started for the bedroom, intending to throw their things into the shopping bags and hustle her charge to a controlled hospital environment. Charlie pulled her up short.

"Wait a minute. We know this bug caused my life support system to fail, but we don't know how it got into the system in the first place."

"We can worry about that later, Stone. Right now, my main concern is your health. We're going back to the base."

"Negative, Remington. We're not going anywhere until we figure out how a mutant strain of bacteria developed in a lab in California was pumped into a plane home-based in Turkey."

"That could take days!"

His jaw set. "So it takes days."

"Be reasonable, Charlie. We'll have to recreate the whole chain of custody for U-2 life support equipment, from the time it left the Lockheed plant to the time it arrived in Turkey."

"Your friend said your boss had wrangled the CIA's cooperation to retrieve certain records. We'll just add a few more items to the request list."

"A few! Unless the CIA has archived everything onto computer disks, they'll need a moving van to haul all those boxes of records."

"That's their problem. While you're at it, ask

your pal to verify Irwin Goode's present where-abouts. I might just decide to pay the esteemed doctor a call.''

"Over my dead body," Diana muttered, shagging a hand through her hair. She took a turn around the room to marshal her arguments, then halted in her tracks. A mask had dropped over Charlie's face, leaving it taut and strained.

Like a hissing cat with fur ruffed and fangs bared, fear clawed its way up Diana's spine. "Are you feeling dizzy?"

His throat worked. Jaw tight, he forced out a single harsh syllable. "No."

"Then what...?"

"I'm sorry, Diana. I didn't think, dammit!"

"About what?"

"About your dead body."

"Huh?"

Ignoring that less than intelligent response, he wrapped a hand around her upper arm and hustled her toward the door. "Forget the stuff in the bedroom. We're heading back to the base."

"Charlie, for heaven's sake! What's got into you?"

"A bug," he snarled. "A mutant microbe. And there's a good chance I passed the little bastard to you."

Enlightenment dawned. With it came a welter of confused emotions. Chagrin. Belated acknowledgment. The tiniest touch of fear. Overriding all else was the awareness that Charlie had shrugged off the bacteria's possible effects on his own pulmonary system, but the thought that he might have infected her had put him in a cold sweat.

"Wait a minute!" Diana dug in her heels. "Let me think about this."

"There's nothing to think about. We've got to get you to the hospital, let the docs test your blood."

"Just hang on a sec, will you!"

His jaw set in a way she was coming to know all too well. He looked ready to toss her over his shoulder. From the dangerous glint in his eyes, he might just have worked up enough steam to get past her defenses and pull it off. Hastily, she went into her scientist mode.

"I agree we need to get back to the base," she said with a credible assumption of calm, "but not because I'm worried you might have passed the bug to me or anyone else. Let's look at the facts. I was with you for six days before you woke up, Charlie, and every day since. We've engaged in close physical contact on a number of occasions."

To say the least!

"I haven't experienced any dizzy spells or exhibited other unusual symptoms."

That wasn't completely true, of course. Since the moment Major Stone had opened his eyes and pinned her with his fierce blue stare, she'd experienced all kinds of unusual symptoms, including moments of sexual excitement so intense she'd come close to blacking out.

"You've also been exposed to a number of other personnel," she continued, shoving aside the memory of those hours in Charlie's arms. "No one's reported feeling ill or suffering from dizziness."

"How do you know?"

"For all that the recovery operation was conducted in absolute secrecy, we followed a specific protocol. The team members would know to report any unusual symptoms. Likewise, the personnel cleared to brief you in at Edwards."

The twin blades of guilt and fear knifing through Charlie's gut took a break long enough for him to process her calm assurances.

"All right," he growled. "Let's suppose I haven't passed this bug on to you. Yet. What's to say I won't?"

"There are no guarantees, of course, but considering that we did everything but crawl into each other's skin last night with no apparent repercussions, I'd say the chances of transfer are pretty slim."

"Pretty slim's not good enough."

Not anywhere near good enough. Just the thought he might have infected this brilliant, vibrant woman with a mutant strain of bacteria sent a icy trickle of sweat down Charlie's spine.

He wasn't afraid for himself. He'd flown too many combat missions and strapped himself into the cockpit of too many test aircraft. Like most of his fellow pilots, he'd learned to calculate the odds of survival, then consciously ignore them.

Adding Diana to the equation threw every calculation out the window.

His fists balled. He hadn't prayed in a long time. Not in over forty-five years, as a matter of fact. Yet suddenly Charlie found himself beseeching the higher power who'd preserved him in ice to spread a similar protective shield around Diana.

With a cool look, the object of his prayers wrenched his attention back to her. ''You breathed in this particular bacterium with the oxygen pumped through your life support system. It appears to have been absorbed through your lungs into your bloodstream. Unless someone pumps more of those suckers into the air around me, there's a very low likelihood I drew them into my lungs.''

She was overstating the matter, deliberately downplaying the risk. He didn't need a Ph.D. to figure that out. But her unruffled calm produced its intended result. Slowly, Charlie unbunched his fists.

''Okay, you've almost convinced me.''

She puffed out a relieved breath. ''Good.''

''Almost.''

To his profound disgust, the hand he lifted to curl around her neck shook like a leaf. She must have felt the tremors when his fingers tunneled under her hair, but thankfully refrained from comment.

"I couldn't forgive myself if I caused you hurt, Diana."

"Really?" Her head tilted back a few degrees, until it rested lightly against his hand. Beneath a fringe of dusky black lashes, her eyes glowed cat green. "Are we speaking in the physical or metaphysical sense here?"

All right. He'd stuck his neck out this far. He might as well lay it right on the chopping block.

"Both."

He waited, half hoping and half scared out of his gourd that she'd reciprocate.

"Funny."

The husky murmur raised a new set of chills on Charlie's skin.

"I was thinking something rather similar just a few moments ago."

She wasn't ready to say the actual words. Neither was he, for that matter. They didn't need to. The slow heat that transferred from her skin to his fingertips said it all.

He'd fallen in love once, or thought he had. The cute little army nurse he'd romanced into a brief, passionate engagement had shipped home, hung up her uniform, and ultimately married her high school sweetheart. Right now, Charlie could barely remember her name, much less her face.

His fingers tightened on Diana's soft flesh. Her hair tumbled over his hand in cotton-soft waves. His chest tight, he breathed in the mixture of shampoo, salt spray, and woman that was hers alone. God, he wanted to kiss her!

Uncurling his hand and putting some distance between them took everything he had. He felt as though he was letting go of his lifeline, splashing into a dark, icy sea yet again. He could only pray she'd be there again, smiling down at him, if and when he woke up again.

"Here's the deal," he said, steeling himself against the acute sense of loss just a few feet of separation engendered. "If you're in no imminent danger of contamination, as you insist, we'll head back to the base…with one quick stop along the way."

"What stop?"

"The Lockheed plant in Burbank. It's only a few miles out of the way."

"But…"

"Just one quick stop."

"Charlie…"

"Lockheed developed and produced the U-2, Diana. They probably subcontracted out the life support system, but Kelly Johnson would have maintained the overall production records right there in his Skunk Works. Johnson never gave out all the pieces of the puzzle. If the program's been declassified, as you say, I might still be able to pull a few strings and get access to…''

"The Burbank plant closed years ago, Charlie."

"What?"

"It's true."

"It can't be! Lockheed Aircraft produced some of the world's finest aircraft. Hell, when they started work on the Dragon Lady, they were turning out seventeen P-38s, four B-17s, and six different versions of the Hudson bomber a day!"

"As far as I know, they're still turning out some of the world's finest aircraft," Diana assured him hastily. "But real estate costs in L.A. went berserk in the sixties and seventies, and Lockheed moved their production plant down to Marietta, Georgia. The Skunk Works moved to Air Force Plant 42, in Palmdale. I remember reading about it in the background dossier they gave me on the U-2 program."

Relief swept through him in palpable waves. He didn't want to imagine a world without the creative genius of Clarence "Kelly" Johnson's famous Skunk Works.

Both Johnson and the Skunk Works were icons of his era. A flimsy structure with packing crates for walls and a circus tent for a roof, the facility was originally set up to design and build a new fighter for the Army Air Corps during WWII. Security around the new project was so tight, other Lockheed employees couldn't help but wonder what Johnson was brewing. The inevitable comparisons to the Kickapoo Joy Juice brewed by Andy Capp's comic strip characters in Dogpatch's "Skonk Works" made the rounds, and the name stuck.

Charlie's first exposure to Johnson came in the mid-fifties, when the dynamic engineer designed and built the first U-2 in a mere eight months. In Major Stone's considered opinion, the Dragon Lady was Johnson's finest achievement. And if he knew Kelly Johnson, the engineer's records were far more complete and detailed than those of the CIA.

"Where's this Palmdale?" he asked Diana.

"If we take a different route back to Edwards, it's right on the way."

"Well, what do you know?" For the first time today, Charlie felt as though things were finally aimed in the right direction. "Let's get our gear and hit the road."

A quick call to OMEGA notified the headquarters of the reason behind their relocation. Mackenzie had just arrived back in D.C. Typically, she shrugged off her wasted trip to the west coast and cheerfully promised to send someone out to retrieve the sensors and cameras. She also agreed to advise Lightning of the change in plans.

That task done, Diana joined Charlie in the bedroom. Collecting the various pieces of clothing they'd bought and worn for the past few days strained the limits of the paper shopping bags. The handles broke on one, and the bottom gave out on another when she threw in her still-damp slacks and top.

"Hang on," she told Charlie as he scooped up his toiletries and prepared to dump them helter-skelter into his gear bag. "I saw some trash sacks under the sink in the kitchenette."

She returned with the box of plastic sacks and tossed him a couple. "They're not very elegant, but they'll do the trick."

Bemused, Charlie rubbed the membrane-thin plastic between his fingers. "When did they come up with this stuff?"

Diana paused, taken aback. He'd acclimated so smoothly to the world as she knew it, she tended to forget he'd skipped almost a half century.

"I don't know. Sometime in the early eighties, I think."

"Amazing."

"You wouldn't think so if you worked in solid waste management. That stuff isn't biodegradable. It doesn't decompose," she translated. "As a result of our dependency on plastic products, this generation is about to be buried in its own garbage. But that's another lecture for another day."

Stuffing her wet things into one of the bags, she tossed the rest of her clothing into another. "Ready?"

Charlie cast a quick glance around the room. His gaze lingered for a moment on the bed. When his eyes met hers again, Diana read both regret and a grim reality in them.

"We'll get through this," she promised. "Together. And when it's over, we might just have to come back to this little hide-away and finish what we started here."

A grin worked its way across his face. "Without the cameras."

"You got it."

They were halfway down the crushed shell walk to the car parked in a wash of moonlight when Charlie's own internal systems went on full alert. He didn't know what set them off. Maybe it was the unnatural stillness of the night beneath the unceasing murmur of the sea. Or simply the heightened awareness of a man who senses danger to his chosen mate.

Whatever triggered them, his instincts were primitive, predatory, and all male. His jaw locked. His muscles corded. Eyes narrowing, he slowed his step and searched the rocks on either side of the path.

"Get back to the cottage," he said softly.

"What...?"

"Now, Diana."

He half expected her to bridle at the abrupt command, but suddenly she, too, tensed. She spun around, sweeping the mounded sand with a hard glance just as a stooped, shadowy figure stepped from behind one of the rocky projections a mere ten yards away.

Charlie recognized him at once. The scientist's stooped shoulders and wreath of whispy white hair made him instantly recognizable. And the hand he kept tucked in the pocket of his ill-fitting sports jacket made him infinitely dangerous.

Chapter 13

"Dr. Goode! What are you doing here?"

Diana played it dumb while she did a swift visual of the figure standing in the shadows just yards away. She didn't see a weapon, but the hand he had buried in his jacket pocket warned her not to make any precipitous moves.

"You sound surprised to see me," the scientist replied. "I don't understand why. You've raised a number of questions regarding my work with the initial U-2 cadre. Surely you must realize I would want to answer those questions in person."

"I don't know what you're talking about."

"Come, come, Diana. One doesn't attain the years or the stature I have in my profession without acquiring a number of acolytes. One of the young men I trained now works at the CIA. He couldn't tell me, of course, who had requested copies of my early studies but thought I'd be pleased to know my work was still in demand. It took me a while to trace the requests to you.''

''How did you find us?'' she asked, abandoning all pretenses.

She sensed rather than saw Charlie inch away from her. She guessed instantly he intended to divide Goode's attention...or draw the man's fire.

''It was quite difficult,'' the elderly scientist admitted, ''but I finally pinned down the origination point of an e-mail you sent to a colleague at the Harrell Institute.''

Well, so much for supposedly secure computers! Mackenzie wasn't going to be happy with the fact that the technology touted by its designers as absolutely, positively inviolate had already been compromised. Probably by some pimply-faced high schooler with nothing better to do than hack into top-secret systems.

Another almost imperceptible movement had her praying Charlie wouldn't do anything noble or stupid, like make himself a target to save her.

''What do you want?'' she demanded, trying to focus Goode's gaze squarely on her.

''Surely, it's obvious. I want to... Please, Major Stone, I must ask you to remain quite still.''

"And if I don't?"

"Then I'm afraid you'll force me to a drastic measure I would rather avoid."

With obvious reluctance, the Nobel Prize winner withdrew his hand from his pocket. Diana expected to see a gun. She'd much *rather* have seen a gun than the slender glass tube he clutched in a hand spotted with age.

Her breath left on a hiss. "Is that what I think it is?"

"I doubt you're familiar with this particular derivative, Dr. Remington. The army has strictly controlled information relating to Mycotoxin T-4."

"What the hell is Mycotoxin T-4?" Charlie snarled.

"An airborne biological agent," Goode explained with gentle patience. "A considerably more powerful derivative of Mycotoxin T-2, known in the seventies as Yellow Rain."

"T-2 was banned by the 1975 Biological and Toxin Weapons Treaty," Diana whispered hoarsely. "In its milder form, it inhibited DNA, RNA and protein synthesis. Its more virulent form caused almost instantaneous vomiting and diarrhea, followed rapidly by hemorrhaging and asphyxiation. I..." She gulped in a steadying breath. "I didn't even know there was a T-4 derivative."

"It was developed some years ago," Goode said. "Purely for research purposes, of course."

"Of course."

"I should hate to break the vial and loose it here. Given this breeze, it could carry to some of the other cottages at the resort. Shall we go back inside?"

Her pulse hammering, Diana darted a swift look at Charlie. Moonlight sculpted his face into harsh planes and angles, but she read the same wild thoughts in his shadowed eyes as raced through her own mind.

Time. They needed to buy time. Talk Goode out of whatever desperate measures he'd planned. Get into position for a counterattack...one that wouldn't give him time to smash the glass vial he clutched.

"Walk backward, if you please, keeping your hands where I can see them."

They backed up awkwardly, their footsteps crunching on the crushed shell, the trash sacks knocking their knees. The ocean's roar deadened all other sounds. The rocky cliffs covered with ice plant cut off any view of the beach below. It was as if the world had narrowed to this narrow, moon-washed path and the three people who trod it.

When they reached the small portico that fronted the bungalow, Charlie's knuckles whitened where he gripped the sacks. He was measuring the distance, Diana guessed, preparing to sling one of the bags.

"No heroics, Major. You and Dr. Remington must die, I'm afraid, but do you really wish to release this virus into the air and take an undetermined number of innocent civilians with you?''

Goode said it so calmly, with absolutely no inflection in his voice, that Diana's blood iced over in her veins. She knew then that there'd be no negotiation, no bargaining. Only an agonizing, if mercifully swift death.

''You're right-handed, are you not, Diana? Please retrieve the key card from your purse or pocket with your left hand and open the door.''

Transferring her sacks to her right hand, she reached across her front and into her purse with her left. The clumsy maneuver allowed her to angle her shoulder a few degrees away from Goode. Not enough to block his view and panic him into precipitate action. Just enough to brush her fingers against the watch strapped to her right wrist when she retrieved the key card. One quick jab on the stem activated the chronometer's transmitter.

''You won't get away with this,'' she said, pitching her voice loud enough to carry over the crashing waves and alert whoever was in the control center. She hoped it was Mackenzie. God, let it be Mackenzie! Fumbling the key into the slot, she threw a fierce argument over her shoulder.

''If Major Stone and I die of Mycotoxin T-4 poisoning, you must know suspicion will turn to you, Dr. Goode.''

He waited until she'd pushed the door open and

reentered the cottage to reply. The plush gray carpet, warm woodwork, and cherry pink-and-green chintz didn't feel quite as welcoming as Diana and Charlie moved to the center of the sitting room. Ominously, Goode remained at the open door.

"I see no reason why I should fall under suspicion," he answered calmly. "Although I assisted the army in development of T-2, I took no active part in the design of subsequent derivatives. If I'm asked about your deaths, I shall speculate that you were both grotesquely afflicted by the mutant bacteria in Major Stone's blood."

Anger flowed hot and fierce through Diana, melting the ice that had formed in her veins. "You knew about the mutant bacteria?"

"I spotted the irregularity two days after I arrived at the oceanographic station. It quite taxed my ingenuity to hide it from you and the others on the recovery team."

"You bastard!" she spit.

His gaze went to Charlie. Genuine regret showed on his aged face. "As much as it pained me to destroy a specimen nature had so miraculously preserved, I couldn't allow you to live. I knew you were aware of the early tests I'd conducted on the effects of superoxygenation. I *didn't* know whether you were aware I'd continued the tests after the CIA officially terminated them."

"Harry Simmons had an idea something was going on," Charlie said through clenched teeth.

"Harry Simmons? Ah, yes, your friend, the Lockheed engineer who worked with us in the initial test cadre. Such a shame a man of his considerable talents developed Alzheimer's, isn't it?"

"Harry wrote me in Turkey. Since the program was so highly classified, he couldn't come right out and say what he was thinking. Just suggested I check out the oxygen filtration system next time I had a chance."

His jaw worked. The plastic trash sacks still gripped in his fists shook with the force of his anger.

"I got the letter right before I took off on my last flight."

"Then you went down and I ceased my experiments immediately," Goode said sadly. "You must understand I never meant to harm any of our pilots. Only to broaden our knowledge of how oxygen and nitrogen interacted at high altitudes with regard to human protein synthesis." He turned to Diana in a quiet plea for understanding. "Without that early work, we might never have unlocked the secrets of DNA and genetic sequencing."

His monumental effrontery left her trembling with fury. "Don't you *dare* try to cloak what you did as research!"

A touch of weariness entered his voice. "Please,

no histrionics, my dear. They have no place in science.''

Diana's horrified gaze was locked on the arm Goode raised.

''Wait!''

''I'm afraid I cannot allow you to discredit my life's work,'' he said with genuine regret. ''And as much as I hate to weigh my contribution to science against yours, you must see that a Nobel Prize winner—particularly one with as little time left as I— cannot spend his last, precious years answering questions about early experiments.''

''You're going to spend your last, precious years behind bars,'' Diana hissed, fully intending to inform him that his every word had been transmitted to OMEGA's headquarters. Before she got out another syllable, Irwin Goode swung his arm.

The trash sacks hit the floor. From the corner of one eye, she saw a blur of motion as Charlie dug into his gear bag and whipped out his Colt.

The shot rang out at the same instant the frail scientist hurtled the glass vial in a high arc. Goode staggered back. Grabbed for the door handle. Stumbling out, he jerked the front door shut behind him. The loud slam almost buried the tinkle of breaking glass.

Paralyzed, Diana saw the vial smash against the wall dividing the kitchenette from the sitting room. Before she could breathe, before she could think,

Charlie wrapped an arm around her waist, lifted her off her feet, and literally threw her into the bedroom. He dived in after her, kicking the door shut behind him.

She scrabbled up like a frenzied crab. She didn't have to glance at the night-darkened windows to know they offered no escape. The rocky shore lay a sheer, fifty feet below. The deck, which might have allowed them to shimmy down its supports, opened off the sitting room. Panting, she turned to Charlie.

"The door won't keep the virus out."

"No, but it might delay the little sucker long enough for you to suit up."

Falling on his gear bag, he tore at the zipper like a madman. In a blinding flash, Diana understood that he intended to save her if he could, with no thought for himself. In the same blinding flash, she recognized two immutable truths. She loved him with every atom of her being—which might or might not be invaded by a horrific virus in the next several seconds. More to the point, she had no intention of climbing into his pressure suit and watching him die.

"The rubber seals have disintegrated," he grunted, tugging at the heavy suit, "but maybe I can stuff your wet clothes around the helmet joint and…"

"No!"

Frantically, she grabbed at his hands. Shaking her off, he dragged out the one-piece suit.

"Get in!"

"No, Charlie! I've got a better idea! The trash sacks can protect both of us. Come with me."

Swooping down, she snatched up the box of garbage sacks and raced for the bathroom.

"Diana…!"

"Grab two towels!"

She lived a lifetime in the next few seconds. Two lifetimes. Hers and Charlie's together. If this didn't work… If she'd miscalculated the density of the plastic polymers… If they both wouldn't fit inside…

Yanking out two bags, she nested one inside the other.

"We'll need two more! Hurry!"

His jaw locked, he snatched out two bags. When he turned back, Diana was already in the tiled stall, standing with one foot inside the nested bags. Hopping, she got the other foot inside and held the edges out for him to join her.

"Get in."

"There's not room. You take it and…"

"Get in, dammit."

His heavy foot landed on her toe, but she didn't have time for pain. Lifting her other leg, she made room for his foot, then simply put hers down on top

of his boot. As soon as he'd climbed in, the aeronautical engineer in him took over.

"Stick your knees between mine," he ordered,
"then scrunch down. I'll pull the other sacks over
our heads. If we draw the strings tight, we might
have a chance."

"Wait!"

Hanging on to his arm with one hand, she reached
down and scooped up the damp towels with the
other. By some miracle, they didn't topple over.

"We can hold these over our faces. Just in case.
Now turn on the shower and pull the other bags over
our heads."

Without another word, Charlie wrenched the cold
water faucet to full "on" position. Icy pellets needled Diana's face and neck, then burst into a hard
wash as she helped him drag the last two bags into
place. She bent her knees as much as his body and
the confined space would allow. He did the same,
making sure the edges of the upper bags overlapped
the lower ones before yanking on the plastic draw-
strings.

His abrupt movements almost sent them both to
the tiles. As it was, they ended up mashed together
at awkward angles. Her bottom rode his thigh. His
shoulder jammed her ear. Grunting, he tried to make
more room for her.

Despite the cold water drumming against the
plastic, their dark cocoon heated almost instantly.

Terror, Diana discovered, did a number on body temperature. Struggling frantically, she wedged an arm between their tight-locked chests and dragged up the damp knit tunic.

"Cover your face."

His fist closed over an end of the fabric. Before jamming it against his mouth and nose, he managed to plant a hard, swift kiss in the vicinity of her lips.

"If this works," he growled over the pelting water, "remind me to ask you to marry me."

"If this works," she got out between hiccups of pure, unadulterated panic, "I will."

Diana had no idea how many seconds or minutes or years passed before she remembered the chronometer strapped to her right wrist. Mackenzie's high-tech wizardry had withstood the Arctic cold. Surely, surely it could withstand an icy shower.

"Control!" she yelled through the wet cloth. "This is Artemis. Do you read me?"

With her left hand occupied by holding the mask over her face and her right arm crunched behind her at an odd angle, she couldn't reach the transceiver to switch to receive. Nor did she dare try to wriggle her arm to the front. She might send them both toppling over. Charlie, however, managed to slide a palm along her arm to her watch. His fingers fumbled with the small knobs for a frustrating few moments.

"How does this thing work?" he asked, his voice muffled by the cloth pressed to his face.

"Press the stem twice."

The chronometer gouged into her wrist as he hit the stem with more force than finesse. Given the circumstances, she didn't complain. She waited, her heart in her throat, until Mackenzie's voice leaped through the darkness."

"I've got you! I've had you the whole time. Are you two all right?"

"For the moment. Send a biohazard decontamination team to the resort. Tell them to be prepared to wash down for…"

"For Mycotoxin T-4. They're already on the way, Artemis. Hold on, okay? Just hold on!"

Chapter 14

The biohazard decontamination team burst into the bathroom just about the time Diana's knees were ready to give out. With a shout made tinny by the speaker built into the visored hood of his respirator, the team leader made first contact.

"Dr. Remington! Are you in there?"

"Yes!" Diana yelled above the force of the water.

"Where's Major Stone?"

"He's right here, with me."

"We're coming in."

The water cut off a moment later. Untangling their arms and legs, Charlie and Diana straightened and fought their way out of the trash sacks. A figure swathed from head to foot in a self-contained, silver-coated decontamination suit stood on the other side of the shower door.

"The readings in this room show only minimal toxin levels," he told them urgently, "but we're going to zip you both into body suits and take you out of the cottage before we wash the place down with paraformaldehyde. Got it?"

"Got it."

"Step out of the shower one at a time."

Feeling like a soggy moth sloughing off its plastic cocoon, Diana hopped out of the trash sacks and into the one piece suit held up by two other members of the decon team. Only a few square inches of their faces showed through the plastic visors, but she recognized one of the team members instantly...or thought she did.

"Jack?"

The former marine flashed her a grin through inch-thick plastic. "In the flesh, doll."

"What in the world are you...?"

The heavy weight of a hood dropping over her head cut off Diana's startled query. A second later, oxygen began hissing into the hood and Jack Carstairs, code name Renegade, hustled her toward the bathroom door. She stumbled, clumsy in the protective gear, and twisted around.

"Charlie!"

"He's being suited up," her fellow operative assured her. "Come on, woman, let's get you out of here."

The scene that greeted her outside the cottage could have come right from a Hollywood disaster flick. Helicopters hovered overhead, their powerful searchlights illuminating the night. Police cruisers and fire trucks surrounded the Hawk, jamming the small parking lot. Blue and white strobes flashed. Uniformed personnel bellowed through bullhorns and warned onlookers to keep back.

Jack directed Diana straight to a waiting chopper. It was ready to go, its blades already slicing the air.

"There's a medical team aboard," Jack shouted, jerking off his hood. "They'll stay with you and Stone until you reach Edwards, then you'll have to go into isolation."

Diana knew better than to snatch off her own hood. Until nasal, skin, stool and blood samples confirmed the presence or absence of Mycotoxin T-4 in her body, the suit would contain any pathogens she might have breathed in.

"How did you get here so fast?" she asked, her voice resonating eerily through the mike in the hood.

His white teeth gleamed. "I was in L.A. when Comm put out the call for a decon team. I spent a few hours in biohazard gear in the corps, so I hopped a ride up here with the team. My orders are to take it from here, Artemis. While you're in detox,

I'll track down and settle matters with your friend, Dr. Goode.''

"The hell you will.''

The angry retort spun both Diana and Jack around. Charlie glared at them through the faceplate set into his hood.

"I intend to settle with Goode myself.''

"Sorry, Major. You're going to be otherwise occupied for a few days, if not weeks.''

"Is that right?''

"Yes, sir.''

As Diana knew all too well, Jack Carstairs had left the marines under a cloud of disgrace more than three years ago, but nothing could obliterate the respect for military rank that had been hammered into him during his years in the corps. With his hair glistening dark as night from the heat generated by the protective gear and his back bayonet straight, he addressed Charlie.

"You'll have to accompany Dr. Remington to Edwards and go into isolation. After that…''

"After that?'' Charlie whipped out, making no effort to hide his displeasure.

"After that, you might be busy with other matters.''

Jack shot Diana a sideways glance. A look of pure devilry danced in his eyes.

"Comm relayed a message for you, Dr. Remington. She said that if we got you two out of this, you're supposed to remind Major Stone to ask you to marry him.''

''She heard that little exchange, did she?''

''Evidently Lightning did, too,'' Jack added with a sympathetic grin. ''I understand Comm patched him in during your entire transmission.''

Oh, great! Nothing like dodging deadly viruses and accepting a quasi-proposal with OMEGA's director listening in the whole time!

''You two better climb aboard,'' Jack suggested. ''The sooner you get through the isolation period, the sooner you can, ah, get busy with those other matters.''

From the tight cast to his face behind the plastic shield, Charlie looked ready to argue the matter. Jack stepped up to him, and a look of male understanding on his handsome, rugged face.

''Comm makes a backup tape of every transmission from the field, Major. When she ran the shot you fired and the sounds that followed through a digital enhancer, it was clear you hit Goode. If the bastard's still alive, he can run, but he can't hide. I'll bring him down.''

''If you don't,'' Charlie promised, ''I will.''

The isolation unit on the second floor of the Edwards Air Force Base hospital lacked any pretensions to charm. Cream-colored institutional paint covered the walls, devoid of any ornamentation that could collect germs. The furniture was metal, gray and functional. The linoleum floor gleamed as bright as glass from its frequent swabbings with industrial-strength antiseptic.

A set of double doors with an airlock in between separated the isolation rooms from the rest of the ward. The intercom provided the only direct contact with the outside world. It cackled at regular intervals with instructions for various personnel to report to their station or to patients.

At least the windows provided a glimpse of something other than bland white walls. They looked down across the base and gave Charlie a bird's-eye view of the busy flight line dominated by its two massive hangars. He'd memorized every architectural feature of the two structures in the thirty-six hours since the decon team had burst into the ocean-side cottage.

Hands shoved in the pockets of his blue hospital pajamas, he stood with legs spread and his gaze locked on the hangars. With each passing hour he'd spent at the window, he'd coiled a little tighter inside. Not because of the samples extracted from his body by medical personnel covered from head to toe in protective clothing. And not because of the damned mutant bacteria, which preliminary reports indicated had all but disappeared from his blood.

Because Diana was in the next room, similarly isolated. Every minute that passed, Charlie alternately prayed she hadn't breathed in any of the toxin and cursed Irwin Goode.

Twelve more hours. They had to spend twelve more hours in isolation. The rest of today and part of the night. If neither he nor Diana showed evidence of pathogenic invasion by that time, the docs would feel comfortable giving them both a clean bill of health. In the meantime, worry for Diana was devouring Charlie from the inside out.

He should have trusted her earlier, he thought savagely. Told her about the disintegration of his life support systems while they were still at the oceanographic station. By keeping silent, he'd lulled Goode into a false sense of security—a security Diana had shattered when she'd initiated her inquiries about the scientist's early work. With the perfect clarity of hindsight, Charlie damned himself for keeping his suspicions to himself and trying to go it alone.

No wonder his few communications with the woman in the next room these past thirty-six hours had been brief and focused solely on his medical condition. Despite her isolation, Diana had taken charge of the entire operation, directing the tests, discussing the results with the docs, reverting to her professional role with a vengeance. The warm, willing woman who'd tumbled into his arms during those stolen hours at the cottage had vanished, leaving Dr. Diana Remington in her place.

Feeling like a caged lion, Charlie turned his back on the window and eyed the tray sitting on the bedside table with distaste. Hospital food hadn't improved much in the past forty-five years, but he...

The whoosh of the outer airlock opening brought his head up with a snap. He waited with mounting impatience while a blast of decontaminating air pressure sanitized whoever had entered the airlock. When the inner door opened, he rapped a quick demand at the masked and gowned figure who entered.

"How's Dr. Remington?"

"I'm fine."

With a quick tug, she yanked off her cloth mask and head covering. Her hair tumbled free of the chemically treated cap, bright and shining in the sunlight that streamed through the window.

Charlie shot a quick glance at the clock. "What are you doing here? I thought we still had twelve hours of isolation to go?"

"We do. But I just heard from Jack Carstairs. I thought you might want to hear his report first-hand."

Her treated, long-sleeved gown swishing, she crossed the room and held up her wrist.

"I'm with Major Stone, Renegade. Please repeat your last transmission."

Static jumped through the air. A moment later, the ex-marine who'd hustled Diana out of the resort, made a succinct report.

"Goode's dead."

"When and how?" Charlie demanded.

"We found him in his lab. It looked like he was trying to doctor the gunshot wound to his side when he suffered a stroke. That's the official cause of death, anyway."

"Roger, Renegade," Diana said. "Thanks." She signed off a moment later, shaking her head. "What a sad end to a scientist of his stature."

Charlie couldn't summon the least sympathy for the man. "He was lucky he croaked before they let us out of here."

And now that Goode was no longer part of the equation, he had more important matters on his mind. Threading his hands through Diana's hair, he tipped her face back.

"Are you all right? Really?"

"I'm all right, really." A smile lightened her eyes. "So are you. Your last three blood samples showed no trace of the toxin *or* the bacteria. You're clean, Charlie."

The relief that washed through him at his reprieve didn't compare to the knifing joy at knowing she was safe. Charlie had experienced more than a few moments of sheer terror in his career, but nothing to what he'd suffered while huddled over Diana in those damned plastic bags.

"We only decided to wait the additional twelve

hours as a precautionary measure,'' she told him happily.

His thumb played across her lower lip. ''Those look to be a long twelve hours, blondie.''

The look she slanted him was pure sex. ''I figured I might keep you company for at least part of the time, Iceman.''

''Part of the time, hell.''

He scooped her up, chemically treated gown and all, and crossed the room in two swift strides.

''The airlock doors have observation windows!'' Diana reminded him, half laughing and half breathless at the hunger that planed his face.

''That must be why the room comes equipped with this curtain.''

Dumping her on the mattress, he reached for the accordion-pleated material. With a rattle of metal ball bearings, he yanked the hospital curtain along the curved rail attached to the ceiling. Seconds later, they were once more encased in a cocoon.

''Good thinking,'' she said with husky approval, reaching up to welcome him into her arms.

With a feeling that he'd been released from dark, frozen ice for a second time, Charlie joined her on the bed. A fumbling jab at the buttons on the control mechanism lowered its back to full horizontal.

They rode it down together, mouths locked, bodies straining. By the time Diana lay stretched out under Charlie, the fear and desperate worry that had twisted her into tight knots these past thirty-six hours had disappeared. All that was left was his mouth, his hands, his rock hard body pressing hers into the tangled sheets.

Minutes passed, maybe hours, before he went to work on the tabs and ties that held her protective gown. Diana did her best to assist him, wiggling to one side then the other to rid herself of the scratchy material and the hospital pajamas she wore under it. When he discovered that her ensemble didn't include a stitch of underwear, the delight on his face was something she'd carry in her heart for the rest of her life.

"Have I told you how beautiful you are?" he got out on a growl, his hands skimming her from breast to hip.

"Not that I recall."

"You are," he pronounced between hungry nips, "the most gorgeous creature God ever put on this earth."

He nibbled his way down her throat and back up again while Diana writhed with delicious pleasure.

"You're…not…so bad…yourself," she gasped, running her hands over his sleek, muscled shoulders. "But aren't you forgetting something?"

"Right."

He brought his head up. Bracing himself on his elbows, he smiled down at her. "I love you, Diana. I didn't realize how much until we climbed into those garbage sacks. All I knew was that I didn't want to climb out and face this world—or any other!—without you.''

"Oh, Charlie, I love you, too! I think I fell in love with you the moment you opened your eyes and grabbed my shirttail. After I got over being scared out of my wits, of course.''

"Of course.''

She waited, her love swimming in her eyes, while the smile faded from his.

"Do you need another reminder?'' she hinted broadly.

"I've had some time to think these past thirty-six hours, Diana.''

"Oh-oh. I don't like the sound of this.''

"I think we both have to face the fact that I might not ever fly again.''

"You might not ever fly air force jets again,'' she corrected gently.

"That's all I know how to do. All I've ever done.''

"So you learn to fly something else. Or don't fly at all. There's a whole new world out there, Charlie, one you've barely begun to explore. We'll explore it together.''

"Are you sure?''

"More sure than I've ever been of anything in my life.''

He swooped down, pressing her into the mattress,

but Diana was discovering she was every bit as traditional as any woman from the fifties. She wanted to hear the words.

After a long, drugging kiss, she fought her way through the swirling pleasure and cleared her hoarse throat. "A-hem. You were going to ask me something?"

Grinning, he brushed her hair back from her face. "Will you marry me, Dr. Remington?"

"Yes, Major, I will."

Chapter 15

A pall of muggy July heat hung over Washington D.C., steaming the air and bathing the vehicles that crawled along Massachusetts Avenue in an early afternoon haze. The driver of the tomato-red convertible with the block-long fins and miles of chrome trim didn't seem to mind the heat. After his years on ice, Charlie couldn't get too much sun.

Nor, it had appeared for a while, could the media get too much of Major Charles Stone. Once the news of his astonishing ordeal in the ice broke, he'd been besieged by reporters and talk show hosts. Within days his face and name had become household icons. Like Dolly, the first cloned sheep, he'd made scientific history.

And like Dolly, his turn in the spotlight had lasted only until the next spectacular scientific breakthrough. A mere two weeks after the Iceman made headlines all over the world, Dr. Greg Wozniak had announced that he'd succeeded in thawing out another ice-age mouse. To Charlie's intense relief, a fifty-thousand year-old rodent riveted the world's attention far more than a broken-down pilot.

With the media diverted to new prey, he and Diana did exactly what they wanted to do. After a hurried exchange of vows before a justice of the peace, they took off on a slow, meandering voyage of discovery across the United States. With the Hawk's top down and the wind in their hair, they used the Santa Monica Pier as a jumping-off point to retrace the old Route 66 and explore a world that held magic for both of them at every turn of the road.

Now, one journey was about to end and another begin. Charlie didn't know which unsettled him more—learning to fly a desk as the Smithsonian National Air and Space Museum's new technical advisor for mid-twentieth-century aeronautical vehicles or meeting Diana's mother and sisters. He had a feeling that the woman who'd been one of the first to burn her bra on the steps of the U.S. Capitol would knock him off his feet with almost the same ease as her daughter.

Compared to that long-anticipated meeting, the

stop-off at OMEGA headquarters for an equally long-delayed meeting with the director would be a piece of cake.

"Turn here," Diana directed.

Following her directions, he guided the Hawk down a quiet street lined with chestnut trees and grand old Federal-style town houses. Moments later, he pulled up in front of a three-story building with a discreet bronze plaque mounted beside the door.

"Who's the special envoy?" Charlie asked Diana as they passed through the portal.

"That's the public persona Lightning presents to the world. He's sort of the president's goodwill ambassador to the rich and famous," she explained with a grin. "As if they need goodwill."

After walking up the short flight of steps and passing through a high-ceilinged foyer crowned by a crystal chandelier, they were greeted by a trim, gray-haired matron.

"Welcome home, Artemis!" Beaming, she hurried from behind her ornate, Queen Ann desk and included Charlie in her warm welcome. "I'm Elizabeth Wells, the special envoy's personal assistant. Please, come this way. He's waiting for you."

"Nice lady," Charlie murmured as they followed their guide through a series of anterooms furnished with more exquisite antiques.

"Just don't get crosswise of her," Diana warned.

"She can put nine rounds dead center through a target in less than ten seconds."

Charlie's brows soared, but he barely had time to revise his mental characterization of the grandmotherly woman before she threw open a set of tall double doors. He caught a glimpse of a towering, five-tiered wedding cake centered on a mahogany conference table, then the crowd inside gave a burst of applause.

"Congratulations!"

"Way to go, Artemis!"

Laughing, Diana pulled Charlie into the crowd, rattling off names as she went. He was introduced to a Cowboy, a Digger and a delicate, stunningly beautiful redhead with the incongruous code name of Saber. Renegade he already knew.

"Artemis is a keeper, Iceman," the square-jawed ex-marine advised. "You'd better hang on to her."

"I intend to."

Lightning looked nothing like the mental image Charlie had constructed. From the remarks Diana had let drop, he'd expected a tense, driven operative with the eyes of a hunter. He'd pegged the eyes right, maybe, but not the man's lazy charm.

"The president sends his congratulations," Nick Jensen told the newlyweds with a smile. "He'll have more to say at the White House dinner he and the First Lady are hosting tomorrow night in the

Iceman's honor, but for now please accept his best wishes along with mine.''

Charlie gripped the hand Lightning offered, wondering what the heck Diana's veiled references to the man's ruthlessness were all about. He found out not ten minutes later.

He and Diana were just in the process of cutting into the five-tiered masterpiece when Mackenzie Blair burst through the double doors.

''Hi, Artemis, Iceman. Good to see you two sans plastic trash sacks,'' the raven-haired director of communications tossed out with a grin.

''Good to see you again, too,'' Charlie returned, his smile dazzling enough to make Mackenzie revise her initial impression of the rather formidable Iceman. ''We owe you one for getting that biohazard decon team there so quickly.''

''All in a day's work,'' she answered, blowing him and Diana a kiss as she threaded through the crowd. ''Chief, we've just received a code level communication.''

Lightning skimmed the single sheet she handed him, his brows knitting. Without shedding any of his casual sophistication, he transformed to a man with a single purpose. Cool. Exact. In command. A man Charlie identified with instantly.

''This one's for you, Renegade.''

''What's up?''

''The State Department has just uncovered evidence of possible death threats against Elena Maria Alazar. I'm detailing you to act as her bodyguard. You leave for San Antonio tonight.''

''The hell you say!''

''Comm will fill you in on the details.''

Renegade uttered another, far more colorful oath, gave OMEGA's director a hard look and stomped out. Mackenzie snatched up a piece of cake and followed in his wake.

''Who's Elena Maria Alazar?'' Charlie asked when the dust had settled.

''The niece of the president of Mexico,'' Diana replied, gathering up a good-sized chunk of the frothy confection. ''And unless I'm not mistaken, the same woman who got Renegade kicked out of the marines a few years ago.''

''Oh-oh.''

''I wouldn't worry about Renegade right now if I were you,'' she advised.

''No?'' Charlie drawled, eyeing her. If he hadn't already lost his heart to his vibrant, brilliant scientist, the look of sparkling mischief on her face at that moment would have melted it on the spot.

''No,'' she replied. Laughing up at him with the joy of a woman totally secure in the love of her man, she hefted a piece of wedding cake in one hand. ''Right now, I'd say your biggest worry is that you're about to go into the ice again. *Icing,* that is.''

To the cheers of the assembled undercover op-

eratives, she introduced Charlie to the modern tra-
dition of feeding the groom a piece of wedding cake
in the messiest manner possible.

* * * * *

V *Silhouette*®

INTIMATE MOMENTS™
presents:

Romancing the Crown

With the help of their powerful allies,
the royal family of Montebello is
determined to find their missing heir.
But the search for the beloved prince
is not without danger—or passion!

Available in March 2002:
THE DISENCHANTED DUKE
by Marie Ferrarella (IM #1136)

Though he was a duke by title, Max Ryker Sebastiani had shrugged off
his regal life for one of risk and adventure. But when he paired up
with beautiful bounty hunter Cara Rivers on a royal mission,
he discovered his heart was in danger....

This exciting series continues throughout
the year with these fabulous titles:

Available only from Silhouette Intimate Moments
at your favorite retail outlet.

 V *Silhouette*®

Where love comes alive™

Visit Silhouette at www.eHarlequin.com

SIMRC3

INTIMATE MOMENTS™

Where Texas society reigns supreme—and appearances are everything!

When a bomb rips through the historic Lone Star Country Club, a mystery begins in Mission Creek....

Available February 2002
ONCE A FATHER (IM #1132)
by Marie Ferrarella

A lonely firefighter and a warmhearted doctor fall in love while trying to help a five-year-old boy orphaned by the bombing.

Available March 2002
IN THE LINE OF FIRE (IM #1138)
by Beverly Bird

Can a lady cop on the bombing task force and a sexy ex-con stop fighting long enough to realize they're crazy about each other?

Available April 2002
MOMENT OF TRUTH (IM #1143)
by Maggie Price

A bomb tech returns home to Mission Creek and discovers that an old flame has been keeping a secret from him....

And be sure not to miss the Silhouette anthology

Lone Star Country Club: The Debutantes

Available in May 2002

Available at your favorite retail outlet.

Where love comes alive™

Visit Silhouette at www.eHarlequin.com

SIMLCC